OTHER NAMES FOR LOVE

FARRAR, STRAUS AND GIROUX

NEW YORK

OTHER

NAMES

FOR

LOVE

TAYMOUR SOOMRO

Farrar, Straus and Giroux
120 Broadway, New York 10271

Printed in the United States of America
First edition, 2022

Pattern art by Berkah Visual / Shutterstock.com.

Library of Congress Cataloging-in-Publication Data
Names: Soomro, Taymour, author.
Title: Other names for love / Taymour Soomro.
Description: First edition. | New York : Farrar, Straus and Giroux, 2022.
Identifiers: LCCN 2021061100 | ISBN 9780374604646 (hardcover)
Subjects: LCGFT: Bildungsromans. | Novels.
Classification: LCC PR6119.O664 O84 2022 | DDC 823/.92—
    dc23/eng/20220118
LC record available at https://lccn.loc.gov/2021061100

Designed by Gretchen Achilles

Our books may be purchased in bulk for promotional,
educational, or business use. Please contact your local bookseller or
the Macmillan Corporate and Premium Sales Department at
1-800-221-7945, extension 5442, or by email at
MacmillanSpecialMarkets@macmillan.com.

www.fsgbooks.com
www.twitter.com/fsgbooks • www.facebook.com/fsgbooks

1   3   5   7   9   10   8   6   4   2

For Zubyr and Durdana

I

ONE

FROM HIS CABIN, Fahad could hear his father shouting instructions at someone, his voice so near it was as though he were here beside him, and Fahad flinched away.

The carriage jerked. A whistle sounded twice. Footsteps thudded down the passageway outside. The crowded platform slid past the window. Fahad set his case on the bed. He inspected his bathroom, sliding its door shut so he could turn around. It was narrow as a coffin, with speckled tin walls, a shower hanging sideways on a hook, a rimless toilet. At the bottom of the toilet was an aperture through which the tracks flashed, faster now as the train sped up. The smell of mothballs prickled his eyes with tears, which he jabbed away with his fists.

He wasn't angry anymore. He really wasn't.

Through the closed doors, over the chug of the engine, the whistle squealing, he heard his father call his name, the syllables hard as drumbeats. There was a small high window and through it the lowering sun made a hot square of light on his face.

His father's voice became louder and louder still. Now he must be in the cabin, Fahad thought, must have his hand raised to the latch of the bathroom door. But when Fahad slid the door open, the room was still empty.

It was to punish him, that much was obvious.

The train passed the low sandstone barracks of Karachi's cantonment, a giant cannon on a plinth angled towards him, a fighter plane painted in camouflage propped up mid-takeoff.

Everything Fahad did, his father twisted his mouth at—that his clothes were too tight, his hair too long, that he sat with his knees too close together or his legs crossed the wrong way, that he spent too much time with his mother and his ayah, that he liked to cook and to set a table, that he was charming company to guests, that he was first in his class this year, that he could recite 'The Charge of the Light Brigade' from memory, that he acted in plays, that his voice was shrill. His father was a cannonball, an avalanche, something giant crashing through the jungle. This was what Fahad and his mother said of him in private, one of the little jokes they shared.

And now Fahad was to spend the summer with him at the farm upcountry instead of in London. To stay in Karachi, even that would have been tolerable. Even Karachi seemed like civilisation. The carriage wobbled, and he steadied himself against a little desk that folded out from the wall. They had reached parts of the city he didn't know: tall apartment blocks—one pale green, another purple, a third yellow—gaudy washing slung out over balconies to dry, rusting air-conditioner casements. The train slowed as the track ascended. They were level now with the higher storeys of these buildings. A woman unfurled a bright red sheet like a flag, her arms splayed. She frowned it seemed directly at him and shook her head.

He would sequester himself, keep himself to himself. He wouldn't allow his father to have any effect on him at all. He found in his suitcase the books he'd brought with him— *History 2, Ad Maths: Statistics, Contents, and Meaning, Macbeth,* and, at the bottom of the case, wrapped in his pyjamas, a book he'd taken from his mother's shelf, adjusting the books around it to close the gap it had left: *Dark Obsession,* subtitled *A Passionate Story of Love Overshadowed by Memories of the Past.* On the cover, a man with wavy golden hair, his shirt open to his waist, his chest gleaming like a shield, was turned towards a woman, her chin tilted up at him, her eyes closed, her fingers curling at his shoulder. Fahad opened the book and reread the first line—which was delicious—then closed it, buried it at the bottom of his case, and tucked the case beneath his bunk, pushed the edge out of sight with his toe.

His mother would be packing for London today. Her cases would be open across the bed, her shoes in their shoe bags nestled against one another, her freshly laundered outfits laid out over the bedcover in their plastic sheaths. On the plane, they liked to sit in the seats at the very front. 'So we're the first to arrive,' his mother would say with her little laugh sharp as cut glass. Everyone wanted those seats, but his mother spoke just so to the attendants at check-in. It was never as though she were asking for a favour. Rather that they should want to do her a favour without her having to ask. It was in the tilt of her chin, the way she held their gaze and pressed her perfectly painted lips together, the way she narrowed her eyes and nodded them towards the conclusion she wanted, a conclusion that was somehow inevitable.

Even the London apartment they borrowed from his father's friend—dark as it was, with the musty smell of damp, with shadows creeping up the walls—she'd fling the curtains open, raise her head towards the outside stairwell as though it were glorious sun, she'd plump the tired cushions on the sofa, she'd tidy the crystal ornaments on the side tables, she'd buy tight little bunches of narcissus from the corner shop and arrange bouquets around the house, and it would become somewhere different: their English cottage. And barely a short walk from Harrods.

'Will it be alright?' he'd asked about Abad, once the rage had subsided, once his tears had dried against his pillow, once he had abandoned all hope of changing his father's mind.

'No,' she'd said, touching her papery fingers to his face, smiling sweetly. 'It will be terrible.' And she'd laughed. 'Horrible.' She'd shuddered. And then confessed, 'I haven't been, of course. But when we married, Rafik and I, hordes of them came from there, dark and ragged, and danced, spinning like dervishes, late into the night, shrieking and hollering round a fire like savages.'

'Why did you do it?' he wanted to ask her, of the wedding. 'Why?' he wanted to ask her, and shake her by her thin shoulders.

The train passed within a tangle of motorways, some half-finished, some ending midair, protruding rusting girders from their concrete slabs. Giant trucks queued at a toll station. The train sped beyond them and now, now there was only desert: pale, flat sand dunes to the horizon, an occasional bush of some spidery plant. His heart became loud and knocked urgently against the front of his chest. He imagined Karachi receding into the distance and he had to see it. He ran down the passageway outside his room, to the door through which he'd climbed into the carriage. Its handle was a giant lever, which he gripped, as though he might with all his weight release it. He lowered a window in the door and leaned out as far as he could, the hot air whipping grit at his cheeks and in his ears but all he could see was the rest of the train, the other carriages snaking behind out of a shimmering haze.

He shouted. He cried out as shrilly as he wanted—sounds, not words, that the wind snatched from his mouth, made vanish. But even here, beneath the whup-whup of the wind about his head, he could hear the sound of his father's voice, hear him calling his name, and when he ducked back into the carriage, he heard it once again, more clearly, from the room at the other end of the passageway.

He returned to his cabin, sat on the bunk with a book open in his lap, flicked page to page, the words swimming in front of him, becoming an indecipherable pattern that he followed with his fingertip, often tracing back to the start of a line again, again, again.

'It's a jungle,' Ayah had said of the farm. 'In the grass there are snakes as thick as this.' She had squeezed the fattest part of his arm. 'And wild cats hungry as lions.'

The sun began to set. The windowpane cooled. The room as it darkened became smaller. The sand turned pink and then mauve and, from hills so distant he hadn't seen them before, long shadows reached towards the carriage like incisors.

There were footsteps outside. They came nearer and paused. Then, a rap on the door.

It was the uniformed bearer who had loaded their luggage
onto the train. A slick of grease down the centre of his nose
shone under the bright lights in the passageway. 'Sir has been
asking for you.' He was barely older than Fahad. There was a
tear at the waist of his jacket where the seam had opened up
to loose threads. His eyes flickered round the room. 'This you
must close,' he said. He slipped past Fahad to the window and
began to wind down the blinds. 'There are bandits.'

'There's no one,' Fahad said. 'Not even an animal.'

'You can't see,' he said. He drew the curtain. 'They are
everywhere.' He glanced inside the bathroom. 'It's alright?'
he said. 'You're comfortable? You're happy?' He edged out
but stopped again in the doorway, reached in, and flicked the
desk lamp on. 'Your father is asking about dinner. He says he
doesn't care, he doesn't eat, we should ask you.'

Fahad shrugged. He shook his head. 'Anything,' he said,
knowing it would be terrible, strange lumps of meat swimming in grease.

'Sir is calling you again.' The bearer jerked his head. He
stood aside, waiting for Fahad. 'I can hear him.' He gestured
down the passageway.

Fahad turned, busied himself with his book, but when he
glanced back, the bearer was still waiting.

'He's in the government?' he said.

Fahad shook his head.

'This saloon is for ministers,' the bearer continued. 'He
must know someone. And they don't give it like that. Many
people ask. They say no.' He gestured again.

'I'll come in a bit,' Fahad said.

'He told me, "You bring him." He'll be angry if I go without.'

He stared ahead. 'The cook is with him now. He must be asking what your father wants. There'—he signalled—'he's calling again.'

Fahad paused at the window. He pushed the curtain aside and lifted a corner of the blind. It was too dark to see anything beyond the glass—only a reflection with a slice of his face in it and the shifting figure of the bearer behind him.

'It's like a TV from outside,' the bearer said. 'Sometimes the train stops in the night, and if anyone is there, they see a full picture. Who there is, what they have. Sometimes they pay these drivers to stop. If the salary is only two, three thousand, they offer them ten thousand, twenty. Sometimes they come and you don't even know. But if they don't find what they want, they bring guns, they wake everyone, they break everything.'

The boy scratched his nose. There was an angry red welt to one side of it. 'My father—if he called and I didn't go,' the boy continued, 'he'd give me a slap across the face. But you people are different.' He rubbed the welt with his knuckle and the patch of redness bloomed across his cheek and over the bridge of his nose.

Fahad thought of his bedroom in Karachi, where he could sit undisturbed for hours, longer even if he kept the lights off so it seemed he was resting.

'It's good,' his mother had said, when he'd come to say goodbye, but as though she were talking to herself. 'But you're my bird, my littlest bird.' She'd sighed then and, with a shake of her head, turned away.

He had a list for her of what he wanted from London: a Russian camera that obscured all but the centre of every

image; a countertop ice cream maker; a programme from
Streetcar, which they had planned to see together. She folded
the note up into a tiny square and tucked it into the inside
pocket of her Filofax. 'No,' she said, touching her fingers
to his cheeks, brushing at their wetness with her thumbs.
'You're a man. Almost, almost. And this is why, this is the
reason, this is what Rafik says, and what can I say then? You
have to be a little—' She shook her fist.

There were things he wanted to say but couldn't—a
horrible feeling had swelled in his throat and stopped him
speaking, so he just lowered his head.

'Where does all this come from?' She waved her hand
indiscriminately, at the sheesham dresser, at her vases of silk
and porcelain flowers, at her crystal jars of stem ginger bis-
cuits and the supari they mixed specially for her at the Club.
'From there. The jungle. So then? You must go.'

He pressed his lips tightly together.

'And Rafik? You think he's this, you think he's that. What
is he? He's your father.' He'd felt angriest with her then—for
a moment he'd imagined hitting her, imagined the bones of
her cheek and jaw knocking like dice against his palm—and
remembering it now, the rage bubbled up sour at the back of
his tongue. She'd get just what she wanted.

'You're coming—' The bearer nodded and stood aside to
make way for him.

'I DIDN'T HEAR YOU,' Fahad said, as he reached the room
his father was in.

There were banquettes on either side upholstered in

glossy pistachio green vinyl. His father sat on one, a table folded out over his legs, papers scattered across it.

'Here he is.' His father directed this at a grizzled old man in a shabby tailcoat and matching pants with a tall white hat on his head.

'It's very late,' the man said. 'How is there time to make dinner?'

'There isn't time?' His father motioned as if he might stand, as if he might toss the table and its contents to the ground.

'There's time,' the man said. 'Of course there is.' He clasped his hands in front of him, squinted at his dark feet in his worn sandals.

'He can make whatever you want,' his father said. 'You say anything you like.'

'Yes, baba.' The man perked up. 'I've cooked in the homes of—' He reeled off a list of names. 'Chinese food, English, Irish stew, chow mein chicken.'

'He likes these things,' his father said, and then to Fahad, 'Tell him now.'

Fahad shrugged. The broad window behind each banquette was uncurtained and the panes reflected the room endlessly like a hall of mirrors.

The man continued naming dishes he could make—potato mash, chicken roast, chicken keev, chicken nuggy, beef roast, beef burger.

'I'm not hungry,' Fahad said—though he was so hungry his stomach twisted into knots. 'I probably won't eat anything. I'll probably sleep early.' He pressed his hot palm to his stomach.

'He'll eat,' the cook said. 'I'll make such things he hasn't had. Even if'—he circled his hand in the air—'he's been to all these places.'

Then, he and the bearer slipped away. Fahad turned to the window opposite his father.

'All this, it's for you,' his father said. 'What do I care for it? I'd be happy coming by road or in a passenger train. But I said, "The boy must be comfortable. He must see what it's like—to go in the saloon and everything."' His papers rustled. 'These fancy lights and this cook and bearer and bedrooms. All for you.'

The lamps on the walls were brass and beneath them there were framed prints—the nearest one of a fisherman squatting by a riverbank hauling a net through the water towards him.

Fahad kneeled on the banquette, leaned over the back, and pressed his face to the windowpane. The glass was cool against the tip of his nose, against the ridge of his brow. He cupped his hand over his eyes. 'It's desert all the way?' he asked.

Were those stars in the distance, or was that a town? He imagined him and his father laughing and talking, like his father did with his friends and visitors, gesticulating insistently. He imagined his own voice booming the way his father's did. He imagined their voices booming together so loudly the walls shook. 'It *was* wonderful,' he imagined telling his mother. 'I think I'll go every summer.' He imagined turning away when she talked about the things she talked about— the flower show, the servants, the Club.

He swivelled round, sat down.

'You've seen the farm,' his father said. 'You've been to Abad.'

Fahad shook his head. 'I haven't.' It was odd sitting opposite his father like that, his father's gaze travelling across
his face as though he were looking for something, so Fahad
looked away, at the pictures on the other wall, this one of a
bridge, that one of figures at a bazaar.

'Of course you have.' His father motioned with his fingers over his lap like he was snipping. 'When you had the
business done.'

The carriage swayed, swung violently, tossing Fahad onto
his side.

He didn't want to be here or there, Fahad thought suddenly, not with his father or with his mother. If the train
stopped in the night, he'd get off wherever it was, wade
through the heavy sand in the dark, just to be away.

'Where are you going?' his father said, as Fahad stood up.
'What's there in your room? Sit down. Stay.' His father tidied
the papers in front of him, glanced again at the page that was
uppermost, then continued. 'Always with your mother. Now,
I want to talk to you.'

To Fahad's relief, the bearer returned before his father
could begin. He seemed to have distracted Fahad's father
from his purpose because, as the bearer dismantled the table
in front of his father and removed it, his father fell silent,
rested his chin on his hand, frowned into the middle distance. Fahad wanted to excuse himself. He thought of things
he could say—that he wasn't feeling well, that his tummy
was funny, that he was tired.

'Sit.' His father frowned again.

Another table was assembled now so that it reached from
one banquette to the other. The bearer unfolded a white cloth
over it, with an orange kidney-shaped stain in the centre, and

came and went with plates, with cutlery, with glassware, finally with a bud vase with a single blue carnation in it and a sprig of baby's breath.

THERE HAD BEEN a play at the end of the school year. Fahad had chosen a lead role. He had known he shouldn't take it, but, as he had rehearsed, he had allowed the thrill of the part—those delicate gestures with the heel of his hand like a kathak dancer, that tight-lipped smile, those elongated vowels—to distract him from the reason. But even as he distracted himself, the reason remained—like someone standing behind the bedroom door as he tried to sleep, like a scooter trailing their car on an unlit road at night. And it came closer. On the night of the performance, a terror had panicked him to the point that he couldn't do his makeup or dress, couldn't remember a single line. 'I can't,' he had said, his teeth chattering with a terrible tremor. 'I can't, I can't, I can't.'

'You can.' His teacher had gripped him by the shoulders, had looked him in the eyes. 'It's a part. You just do the part.'

Someone had hurried backstage—a silly girl with a minor role—to say that the corps commander of the city was here, and the president of the Club.

'You are an actor,' his teacher had said. 'You put on'—he had brushed his fingers across Fahad's face—'the mask.' So Fahad had: the wig, the pinafore, the stockings, a dash of red across his lips. And as soon as he stepped on-stage, into the blindingly bright lights, everything fell away from him, even himself, so that he was a ghost, a plume of smoke, an invocation.

At the curtain call, he had received the loudest applause.

Someone had shouted bravo. A few people had stood up. But he had noticed as he took his bow that his father's seat was empty.

His parents hadn't spoken about the play afterwards. Fahad had mentioned it once—to say, tentatively, how much people were talking about it, how well they thought he had performed, how funny they thought he'd been. It was a role, he'd wanted to say. A role was nothing. His father had frowned at him, had studied him closely, hadn't looked away. His mother had told a story about a friend who hadn't been right, hadn't been right at all, how sad it was, how thoughtless, how her family had suffered.

Since then, he'd avoided being alone with his father—which was easy because his father travelled often and had visitors when he was home—and on the few occasions they were alone together, Fahad had filled the silences with mindless talk.

HIS FATHER NARROWED his eyes at him. Fahad gripped the edge of the banquette. 'You're how old now?' his father said. 'Fourteen? Fifteen?'

'Sixteen.' His mouth was dry and the word came out funny.

'Sixteen? At that age my father had passed.' His father held his fork and knife up like he was preparing to eat, but his plate was empty. 'And I was married.'

It wasn't true. His father had married later. Fahad had seen the pictures. Fahad kicked his heels against the seat. He chewed his lip till he tasted blood. 'It isn't true,' he wanted to say. 'It was for school,' he wanted to say. His face became hot and he bent over his lap.

'I can talk to you then as if you are a man,' his father said. 'You *are* a man.'

Something jittered in Fahad's chest—why?

'Uncle is dead,' his father said, putting down his knife and fork. 'Mumtaz Chacha.'

'Your uncle,' Fahad said.

'But he was like a father to me.' His father shook his head. 'Mine was gone.' He steepled his fingers under his chin. 'I wanted my father's seat. I was entitled, of course. But Uncle said, "No, no, you're a bachha, you wait your turn." It *was* my turn. The son inherits from the father. This is how it is. And with the seat, with my father's name, I'd have been a minister. I'd be a minister now. But Uncle said, "When you're ready, the seat will be yours. I'll keep it warm for you." He gave me the lands, the farm. To keep me busy.'

His father continued talking—not about the play, not about Fahad, about other things. 'But what did I know of farming? And it was too much for anyone. It was not a farm, it was a jungle. There were hills'—he reached his hand to the ceiling—'and ditches. There were forests, wild animals. And I had no money.'

The bearer and cook appeared with trays laden with tureens. The cook arranged the tureens in front of them—one, another, a third, a fourth, a fifth, a plate of rotis, dishes with different kinds of pickles. He indicated one with his little finger—the nail of which was stained red. 'Green mango.' He removed the lids of the covered dishes, each time with a flourish, announcing each like the arrival of a guest.

'I wanted the seat, not the farm,' his father said. 'My father had said this to me. "Your plate is always full," my father had said. "But these people of Abad, how many go hungry?

You go where you want, but where are the roads for the peasants? If you get sick, there is someone to care for you, but what do they have? No doctor, no hospital." He made me promise. "After me, it is for you, for you to give them these things. I gave them to you, and you give to them, and they will give you their vote. They don't know even what it is. They'll put their thumbprint where you tell them. Because of my good name. You understand?"'

Fahad inspected the contents of the dishes.

'What could I do?' his father said. 'Uncle was my elder. He had all the money. I had none. I couldn't have fought an election with the pocket money he gave me every month. To myself, I said, "One day, Rafik. Not today, but one day you can say for yourself what you do." Uncle said to me, "What you make from the farm, you can keep half." Half the land was my father's. Half the income was mine by right.' His father struck the table with his fist. 'And it was a jungle. How was I to make money from it? I needed money to cultivate it. I borrowed from every friend of my father. I levelled the earth.' He swiped his hand like he was slicing off somebody's head. 'I made paths. They thought I was mad, the people there.'

Fahad agitated a gravy with a ladle, prodded a joint with the point of a knife. In fact, the rotis were parathas—lacy and delicate as handkerchiefs. Some were stained dark and filled with bitter methi leaves, some were golden, layered with slices of potato so thin they were translucent.

'And the records I kept,' his father continued, 'a ledger with a separate entry for each farmer. For each farmer!' He rapped his knuckle against the table. 'I would show it to Uncle, and he would say, "Take it away." He would refuse to look. "Trust," he would say. "Because of trust." He was a fine man in his own way. A man's man.' He paused. He tilted his head, narrowed his eyes at the window.

There were fried hunks of sweet river fish, spiked with bones fine as needles. There were fibrous pinwheels of lotus root stewed in mince. There was a leg of roast lamb, studded with cloves, cinnamon, and cardamom, its meat gelatinous, melting away from the bone between Fahad's fingers. He dabbed at the corners of his mouth, where the spices burned, with a scrap of roti. His father talked about family and politics and the extraordinary power of his father's name, of his uncle's name even, that people approached him at airports, at weddings, at funerals, to tell him the things his uncle had done for them, the job he had got them or the transfer or the court hearing. 'What do I care for power? Power is not something one pursues. Power pursues the man. And if it comes, then what?'

Fahad shrugged.

'Responsibility. Great responsibility. This is what history tells us. You should be learning this.'

'I am.'

'Churchill. Churchill teaches us this.'

His father barely ate, pushing his food around his plate with his fork, furrowing lines through a pile of rice, through a streak of saalan. 'The father, the son. This is the question, isn't it?'

Fahad froze. But his father seemed far away in his thoughts. He was looking at Fahad but not looking at him.

'But the son takes no interest,' his father continued—and Fahad realised he meant his uncle's son, who lived in London and occasionally sent Fahad gifts, a brightly coloured tie last year, a tasselled silk scarf the year before. 'He doesn't take responsibility, not for the lands, not for the people. So then? Who must do it?' He knocked his fist against his chest.

The cook returned to refill the empty dishes and complained that Fahad had not tried the brain or the trotters. 'These boys are always hungry—' He patted Fahad on the shoulder and Fahad felt an unexpected affection for him.

Fahad continued to graze, helping himself directly from the serving dishes with his fingers, to the bitter gourd, the crisp fried okra, another morsel of fish.

His father had never spoken to him so much before.

'But, and this is important, now you must pay attention. For the farm, you must have the seat.' His father clapped his palms together. 'They are like this. You cannot keep a farm such as ours, the largest in the province, unless you have the means, unless you pull the strings.'

'Why?' Fahad said. It wasn't vinyl on the banquettes. It was glossy leather that creased softly as he leaned into it.

'Why?' his father said. 'These people are thugs. They're goondas. They'll take it from under you, take the water from your canals, make trouble between your villages. The things a man has of value, he must protect them.'

After the plates had been cleared, the cook brought dessert: a soup of evaporated milk with cubes of jelly in neon colours—pink, green, orange—bobbing in it, scattered with flaked almonds. It was his speciality, he said. There was ice cream in it too.

His father filled a bowl. 'Yes?' he said. 'You're understanding better now'—crystals of jelly glittered in the well of his mouth and between his teeth—'the ways in Abad. You and your mother want me to be easy like this'—he swayed to one side, then the other—'like that. Your mother says, "Be like the reed that bends in the breeze." In London there are reeds. Here there are none. Here there is jungle. Here you must—' He sliced his hand through the air.

It was almost as though they were friends or peers, the way his father was talking to him. It made Fahad feel big himself, as though he took up all the space on the bench. He leaned his head back. It was too heavy to hold upright. There was a bottle of Scotch on the table now, an ice bucket too and tumblers. His father prepared a drink for himself.

FAHAD WOKE IN THE NIGHT. Though the train had stopped, he still felt its motion thrumming through his body, his body bracing against the bed. Through the wall, he could hear a low rumble, a sound like distant thunder, that came and came again and he realised that it must be his father snoring, as though they were side by side. He climbed out of bed. He parted the curtain. He wound up the blind. It was dark outside—but a lighter dark, a dark that had some shape and colour. He waited and listened.

TWO

A GREAT MANY PEOPLE were at the station to receive Rafik—in addition to his staff, several millers he knew, townspeople, a mid-level government official, some of his farmers. Karachi was a fine city—with its restaurants and beaches, with its grand old families in their grand old homes—but he could never feel for it as he felt for Abad. What was it about the place? It had a heat this time of year that bowed a man's head—unashamed, unrestrained, unmediated by office blocks and blacktop roads, untempered by Karachi's sea breeze. And a familiarity amongst the folk as though they were blood: the crafty stationmaster, who had wrested Rafik's bag from his manager to carry it to the car outside to be sure of a tip; the legless beggar on his sled in the station hallway who lowed in recognition as Rafik tossed ten rupees into his lap; his old driver, who had been his father's driver, who had taught Rafik to drive on his knee when he was a boy and who now fought with the stationmaster to load his bag into the dickie.

They *were* blood, these people of Abad, bonded together

across generations, to the earth they tilled, the water they channelled across it, the seed they sowed, the grain they harvested. They had eaten the salt at his father's table, at the tables of his forefathers. Now they were sons to him, all of them who lived here, like he had been his father's son, his uncle's son, the son of his elders, all gone. It was why he had acceded, of course he had, to his uncle's wish that he look after the farm, that he take the seat only after his uncle was gone. It was why he had spent millions levelling the lands, cutting the jungle away, making these plains fertile, turning the grey sand green, then gold. It was love, it was loyalty, it was honour. It was what made a man a man.

And though the only road through the town of Abad was a dirt track, though open sewers ran alongside and men had nowhere to shit but in the shade of a wall, like this fellow they were passing here, though the rubbish collected in mounds at every corner, though the road was still stained from the Edh sacrifices weeks ago, though the children had nowhere to play but in the street, streaking after a ragged dog or punctured football, his heart swelled with love, with pride, with duty—yes, duty—to be here.

'And?' said the old driver, who took the privilege of speaking to Rafik informally, as he'd known him as a child. 'You didn't bring the baba? Little Fahad? Doesn't he belong to us as well?'

Then Rafik remembered and shouted at the driver to stop, no, why was he stopping, the fool, turn back. 'And you,' he told his manager. 'Hurry, run, run and see, he must have forgotten to come after us, to get off the train, even.' Always in his room, never listening to what was being said, never seeing what was happening, this was why he had to bring the boy here. To grow him up. His mother keeping him a baby, even holding him in her arms like a child, though he wasn't at all, he was a man, he *was*, he was a man. And what way was this for a man to behave? To lock himself up like a woman in purdah.

His manager was gone so long Rafik sent the old driver after him. A good while passed till he saw only the servants returning. He thought about whom he'd have to call, that he should have tipped the stationmaster better, that the boy would be fine, really he would, he probably wouldn't have noticed, wouldn't have left his cabin, and he wasn't such a child anyway, but Rafik imagined him as a child, those thin arms all bone. The driver and manager parted as they approached the car and behind them was the boy, waving his hands and shaking his head, like a mad thing.

'What is it?' Rafik said. 'What's wrong? We were waiting. We didn't go anywhere.'

The boy slapped at his own face. 'The flies.' He tore at the collar of his shirt. 'They stick, they're everywhere,' he said. 'Even inside.' He reached, scrabbling, into his shirt.

They got him into the car.

'In my mouth too.' The boy wiped his mouth against his sleeve, clawed into it with his fingers.

The manager wound his window down and waved the flies out—there weren't so many at all. 'There aren't so many at all,' Rafik said. 'It's no different from anywhere else.' After a moment, he added, 'You always stay in your room, and you don't see what's happening. It's dangerous. You must be alert. You must listen. You must look. This isn't Karachi. Even in Karachi you must.'

A passer-by saluted at the car, and another, seeing him

salute, saluted as well. 'Now you also raise your hand,' he told Fahad. 'People are happy to see us.' He pointed out the sites—the old clock tower, the Christian cemetery. 'You think of these folks as your family. Your family to care for. What does a man do?'

The car slowed and then stopped. A junction that was always crowded was crowded now, the traffic at a standstill, a van parked diagonally where the four roads met, loading people into the back, the driver hanging out of his open door without a care in the world, unknotting the curls in his beard, calling for passengers to Shikarpur, Sukkur, Naushahro Feroze, as merrily as though he were singing a song. A truck of wheat could not pass. A donkey cart for which there was no room had driven into an impasse head-on with a tractor. The traffic warden bobbed like a buoy in the midst of it all.

'You see,' he told Fahad, 'how they are here? Fighting with no sense, no sense at all. This is another responsibility. When my father was in power, there were announcements at every traffic light.' He shouted at the van driver to move and the man waved leisurely at the women in their faded burqas bundling into the back.

'Who is this idiot?' Rafik said. 'I'll give him a slap.'

His manager climbed out and disappeared behind a rickshaw. He reappeared a distance away, collared the traffic warden, gestured back, no doubt explaining that Rafik was in the car, was waiting and shouldn't be. The warden squinted in his direction, salaamed, hurried towards the van, shoved the driver in, slamming the bonnet with his open hand. The donkey cart attempted to move into the space the warden had left and Rafik's manager obstructed him, arms outstretched.

The warden and his manager guided the traffic, someone jumping off the back of the truck to do the same.

'It's like a puzzle,' Rafik said, space beginning to clear. As they passed the van, Rafik swiped at the driver through his open window and when he caught him on the ear and the bastard hollered, he looked for the boy in the rearview mirror to see that he had seen. 'This is the way,' Rafik said, 'not the reed but the jungle.' The boy had shrunk into the corner of the back seat. 'You can't see anything like this,' Rafik said. 'Sit up. Look from the window. We're out of the town. Where the town ends, our lands begin. Don't you want to see?'

At the police chowki that marked the municipal boundary, the officers stood up to welcome Rafik. 'These rascals,' Rafik said. 'If we were ordinary folk, they'd be blocking the way so they could take a bribe.'

The boy was sitting up now, staring cautiously from a corner of the window.

Rafik explained to him the work the farmers were doing. 'The transplantation,' he said. 'They take the seedlings one by one and they put them in the field.'

'Why?'

'This is the way. How pleasant it is to see. It makes'—he patted his chest—'the heart feel full.' Women and children fanned out across the flooded fields, the water a rippling sheet of gold, with the seedlings bundled on their backs, wedging one stalk into the mud at a time by its wadded roots. 'The men are lazy. You won't see them. All drinking in their villages.'

'Are there snakes?' the boy said.

'There's everything here,' Rafik said. 'Whatever you want.'

'Only a few are bitten,' the manager said. 'Not so many die, but in this season more.'

'And wild cats?'

'It was jungle,' Rafik said, slapping the dashboard. 'This was what I told you, when my father passed. My uncle said, "You do what you want but there's no money." I borrowed. Every friend my father had, I joined my hands together, I said, "Unless I level it, I can do nothing with it." They thought I was mad. They said it's good for hunting, nothing more.' Some of the farmers clambered up onto the verge to salute the car as it passed. 'I spent millions. I thought, "What will I do if they're right, if it makes no money?" I didn't know the first thing about farming. I was your age. I was a boy.'

'Your father, the work he did, it brought tears to people's eyes,' the driver said into the rearview mirror. 'They cried to see how hard he worked. Himself in the fields. The mud up to his knees.'

'And the first season, you remember?' Rafik continued.

'Everything died,' the driver said. 'There was a plague of locusts from the north.'

'My uncle said, "What have you done? You've borrowed from every friend I have. How will I repay them?" Of course there was money. He didn't want to spend it. But I said, "I must try till I succeed." How I had the courage, I don't know. And the second season, we did well, and after that, better and better. Twenty-four villages now across the lands. Think—five hundred, a thousand living in each village. You add it up. So many lives that depend.'

At the turning for the house, more farmers had gathered and they cheered, those who carried sticks waving them in greeting. The arch across the track that led up to the house was obstructed by a ladder, a man at the top with a brush.

'Who is this?' Rafik pointed to the face painted on the left column of the arch. 'Your grandfather. And this?' He pointed to the right column. 'Your uncle. And in the middle?'

'I don't know,' the boy said sullenly.

'Your father,' his manager said.

'It doesn't look like you,' the boy said. 'The eyes are too big.'

'They haven't finished it,' Rafik said. And then to his manager, 'See how they do it.'

To pass, the car had to drive over the verge into the adjacent field and then up again. The tyres raced in the dirt, earth spraying up around them, clods knocking against the chassis, and then the car skidded back onto the track, narrowly avoiding a tree.

Rafik pointed out the low whitewashed wall of the house to the boy—at the end of the avenue of neem trees and round the bend. 'You'll like it,' he said. 'It's a special place.' It was good he'd brought him. It was. How else would a boy learn than from his father? 'You'll make friends here,' he said. 'It's not so easy at school for you, your mother says.'

'It's fine,' the boy said quickly.

'You're tired now,' Rafik said. 'Tomorrow we'll go everywhere, around the lands, village to village.'

MANY HAD COME to the house to welcome him—more perhaps than had come to his uncle's funeral only a month ago—already, of course, asking for favours. 'I have no position as yet,' he told them. 'Let me have the seat, let me join

the government, then I can see what to do.' But still, they
wanted him to call the chief of police or the dean of this
college or the surgeon at that hospital. 'Baba, give it time,'
he told them. 'When I have a cabinet position, these officials
will do anything we want.' But he was happy to find that the
officials he called answered and listened nonetheless. 'This is
the work we do,' he told the boy. 'People think it's a thing to
fight for. It's a job. A hard one.'

The boy seemed to enjoy the attention, all the staff waiting on him hand and foot, all the visitors asking about him,
why he hadn't come sooner, when he'd come to Abad to
live, when he'd learn the language and, of course, when he'd
marry—at which the boy blushed like a girl. 'It's nothing
to be ashamed of,' Rafik said. 'Everyone does it. Even the
birds and the bees.' And he nudged the boy in the ribs and
winked.

'All good, all well,' he told Soraya when she called from
London. 'Settling in grandly. He didn't want to share my
room and the guest room they're still fixing, so I put him on
the landing where there's a bed. No AC, but he said he was
happier there. Good for him to have the company of men.
Learning from you all these bad habits. These nakhras.'

IN THE MORNING, Rafik took the boy to the lands. 'You see
now all that your father has done.' The boy wasn't happy
in the little jeep, squashed into the back with the manager
and others. 'We cannot take the big car,' Rafik told him. 'The
roads are too narrow. And there weren't even roads before. I
said, "There must be access to every plot of land. I must be
able to see it." Why? They're all crooks. They'll say one thing

and do another, so unless you see it with your own eyes, you won't know. I'm teaching you.'

He was clever though, the boy. Quick to learn. He asked about this and that—what were those squares of grass? Why were some fields flooded with water and others dry and rocky?

'These are the seedbeds.' Rafik stopped the car and they all piled out so that he could show the boy, who stroked his hands through the stalks, lush as an animal's pelt. 'From here they take each stalk one by one and put them in the field. When they're ready to do that, they open these channels you see here on the sides.' He showed him the narrow earthen courses that ran alongside the fields. 'And they let the water in. Until the stalk turns yellow, the rice must be so high in water.'

They returned to the car and continued on. 'See, I can access every piece of land. As far as you can see in every direction, it's ours. You won't find a farm like this anywhere in the district, even the province. They say you shouldn't be proud. Of course I'm proud. I worked hard.'

The boy asked about the birds— the white long-legged ones wading through the flooded fields, and the ones with black feathers and bright blue tails that darted from the boughs of the trees along the canal down to the water's surface.

'All local types,' Rafik said. 'We can find out the names for you.'

The canal was brimming with bronze, silty water and the bank on which they drove gleamed with wetness. The farmers' wives were dotted across the fields like jewels in their bright clothes.

'I'm happy you're here,' Rafik said, surprising himself, not because he wasn't, only because the feeling was unfamiliar.

He took the boy from village to village. 'You learn the

name of each,' he said. And at every village, children came running out to greet them, jostling past the elders, screaming and shouting, clamouring at Rafik's window, where he distributed toffees from a large canister he kept in the back.

He showed the boy Bibi's temple between two of the villages. 'You see that little patch,' he said, 'with the trees. When I cleared the forest, the people stopped me. They said, "You do what you want, it's your land, but this field you cannot touch, because a saint is buried here." I argued and argued, but they set up their homes here to stop me, so I couldn't bring my tractors. Finally I went to our spiritual leader. I asked him. He came, he looked all over. He said, "Yes, a saint is buried here. But only here. You leave this"—he marked it with stones—"the rest you do what you like with it."'

'What kind of saint?' the boy said.

'They call her Bibi,' Rafik said.

'She was very wise,' the driver said.

'She died very young,' the manager said. 'Women who couldn't have children, they went to her.'

'Every tree looks different,' the boy said. 'Is that how the jungle was?'

A light flashed beyond the trees and then a car appeared from behind the temple, sunlight sparking off the bonnet. It was a jeep like Rafik's, but newer and bright green. It continued along the parallel track. Rafik asked and they told him it was his cousin, Mumtaz Chacha's son.

'It's Mousey,' he told the boy. 'Come for his father. Good he's having a look, taking an interest. Before he goes back to London, he can see all the work it is for me to manage.' They watched till the jeep turned away and then he ordered the driver on. 'Nobody knew who he was, poor fellow, at his father's funeral, sitting in the corner. I took them over to meet him. They said, "We didn't know there was a son. We thought it was only you." "He's been in London all his life," I said. "He's from there now."' A farmer waved their car down to complain about a dispute. 'What is there in London that is so good? Shopping—is this what you and your mother do? What kind of thing is it to do?'

'We do lots of things,' the boy said.

'He was like this always,' Rafik said, still thinking about Mousey. 'At school, he was younger but we were in the same class.' They stopped to allow a convoy of buffalo—their wet hides glistening like onyx—to cross the path. 'Always I'd tell my friends, if you are my friends, you are his friends. If you invite me, you invite him. They didn't want to. "He doesn't talk," they said. "He's quiet. He's not right." "He's perfectly a-one," I said. So everywhere I went, I took him, like you take your schoolbooks.'

The track that led to the last village was lined with young date palms. 'This lot are very enterprising,' he told the boy. A pair of wild dogs yapped at the car and the boy shrank back from the window. A crowd of children was waiting by the earthen wall. 'They waste nothing,' Rafik said, showing the boy the dung bricks patted against the wall to dry. The children pressed up against Rafik's window, screeching when he pulled the canister of sweets out from under the dashboard. 'Here.' He handed the canister to the boy in the back. 'You give it,' he told him.

'It's okay,' the boy said, not taking it, the canister suspended in the space between the headrests.

'They'll be very happy,' Rafik said. He pushed the canister and after a moment, the boy took it.

'What should I do?' the boy said, as they all piled out of the back.

The manager arranged the children into a line alongside the car, with the boy at the head of it. The boy unscrewed the lid and cautiously held out a handful of toffees.

'You see,' Rafik said. Smoke spiralled up from somewhere inside the village and a pair of goats skittered, bleating, across the yard. The noise of the children became loud and then his manager began shouting too. The children had surrounded the boy, who had disappeared beneath them, all of them grabbing at once, the canister bobbing between them, now tilting onto its side, now emptying entirely.

Rafik reached through the open window to slap at them and his manager wrenched them away by their necks or, for those who were clothed, by their collars. The boy was cowering in the centre, his elbows over his head.

'You're wild,' Rafik shouted. 'I'll beat you with my bare hand.' His manager hit out at the few who hadn't scattered and then coaxed the boy back into the car. 'You have to hold it tightly,' Rafik said. 'You can't be so soft like you are doing your play, all this and that—' He turned his wrist in the air. 'You have to be tough. You have to show them. They want to see who is the boss. Who is?' The boy said nothing. He had a scratch across his cheek. 'It's alright,' Rafik said. 'Don't make a fuss.' The boy's shirt was torn along the placket. 'Come on now,' Rafik continued. 'Next time you show them.'

'I didn't want to do it,' the boy said, curling his head towards his knees, his voice warbling.

'It's alright, it's alright,' Rafik said. 'No need to cry and shout about it.'

They made the rest of the journey back to the house in silence.

RAFIK DIDN'T SLEEP terribly well. He woke up thirsty in the middle of the night and then dropped the glass he was drinking from in his dressing room, where it shattered. Amongst the pieces, he found the base of the glass, which had split cleanly in two—a crescent and the shape that fitted against it. He held them together, up to the pale light coming from his high, narrow window.

In the morning, he remembered the neighbour of his with a little land, with the Shell pump on the outskirts of town. He had a son about Fahad's age, a tough, local sort. A good example for the boy. He called them to the house, sat with them in his bedroom. 'He's a clever one,' he told them about Fahad. 'Always reading. Even now if you go upstairs he'll be with a book.' He butterflied his palms in his lap to show them. 'He's grown up with women,' he continued. 'The ayah, the mother, fussing, fussing, fussing.'

'You should keep him here,' his friend said. 'Full time. Get a teacher, he can learn his lessons at home. And meet people. People can see him. So one day he can take over from you. Otherwise, what will you do?'

'This is what I'm saying,' Rafik said.

'The daughter may stay with the mother,' his friend went on, 'but the son must be with the father. Look—' He gestured at his own son.

Rafik sent the bearer to get Fahad. He returned, saying the baba would come. 'Tell him now,' Rafik said. He followed the bearer out and shouted up from the stairwell. Then, after some minutes, the boy appeared, dragging his feet, his hair and clothes as though he'd been sleeping. 'You should tidy yourself,' Rafik said in his ear as they went back into the room. 'This is what a man does.'

'Here he is,' his friend said, standing, clapping Fahad on the back, the boy limp as a fillet. His friend introduced his son, who was broad and sturdy, a thick beard down to his chest even at his age.

'How old is he?' Rafik asked.

'Seventeen,' his friend said.

'They're the same,' Rafik said. 'He'll teach you very well,' he told Fahad, 'what all you need to know here.'

Again Fahad didn't speak a word, sat looking at his knees, at his hands, for some great wisdom in them. 'This one'— Rafik patted him on the leg—'knows everything. You ask him any question, he'll tell you the answer.'

'I don't,' the boy said.

'Anything,' Rafik said.

'You learn the language,' his friend said to Fahad. 'You learn the customs. This is most important of all. This is your home. The rest—what does it matter?'

'Good, good,' Rafik said. 'Now you two have met,' he told the two boys, 'there can be a friendship like I have with your father.'

'When we were children we played in the canal,' his friend said. 'You remember? They'd throw us mangoes to eat, we'd suck the seeds dry and toss them behind us.'

'He was the greediest,' Rafik said. 'Three, four mangoes he'd eat quicker than I could have one. And now see—' He nodded his head at his friend's round belly, and they laughed.

The bearer announced another visitor.

'He can wait,' Rafik said. 'Who is it?'

It was Cousin Mousey.

'Of course, of course, why didn't you bring him in? This is his home. You don't have to tell me.'

Mousey was a funny one—entering the room head bowed like a servant. Rafik slapped him playfully. 'It's alright for London but over here only the Hindus are clean-shaven,' he said. They talked about Mumtaz Chacha.

'Such men you don't find anymore,' the friend said. 'A man's man. Liked by all.'

'By all,' Rafik agreed. 'And not afraid to be tough. Tough as nails.'

'And he liked all as well,' the friend continued. 'My father before he died, he said, "Our votes will always go to Mumtaz. We are the children and he is the father."'

'What children are you?' Rafik said. 'Ten thousand votes,' he explained to Mousey. 'Not children at all.'

Mousey and Fahad had always got on—and now they talked softly, almost privately, Mousey asking about school, about some book, about Soraya, telling him something about London, about this play or that museum.

Tea was brought. Mousey refused a cup. 'You cannot say no,' Rafik told him. 'This is our way here and to say no is an insult. A grave insult.' He laughed.

There were some things to discuss, Mousey said.

'Yes, yes,' Rafik said. 'All ears.'

Mousey looked at the friend, made a soft noise like he was thinking aloud.

'You're forgetting who this is,' Rafik said. 'A brother to us. We played in the canal as children. You remember?'

'You remember?' The friend reached across to squeeze Mousey's knee.

'Whatever you want to say, feel most free,' Rafik said. 'Absolutely free.'

Mousey had a strange way about him—seeming more like a boy with his hair cut so close and his clothes that didn't fit. He looked again at the friend, at the friend's son, then removed the tissue box from the table and shifted the tea-cups. He took a roll of paper that had been tucked under his arm, spread it out on the table. It was a map, a section coloured green, another blue, an area divided into smaller plots, a jagged line through the middle.

'Aaaah,' Rafik said. It was the lands. This was their canal and here, branching off it, the watercourses. Here were the warehouses, here the temple, here the uncultivable low-lying fields. 'Very good,' he said. 'Very useful. It was all jungle.' He spread his palm across the sheet to show Mousey. 'All of it. I cut down the trees. There were hills and ditches.'

Mousey nodded.

'Day and night he worked,' his friend said. 'Day and night. The mud up to here.' He levelled a hand halfway up his leg.

'Higher,' Rafik said. 'Much higher.' He pressed his finger into the green section. 'So what is this colouring system?' he asked.

'This shows'—Mousey shifted one way, then the other—'what is yours and'—he indicated the blue—'what belongs to me.'

'Mine and yours?' Rafik said, sitting back, then forward again, then back. 'Ah, that's not possible to tell. If I took a handful of soil from one place and another and I mixed it'—he mimed, cupping his palms together—'how can you say yours and mine? No, no, you leave all this business alone.'

Mousey looked at his knees, looked at the map.

'It's good what you're doing,' Rafik said. 'You're taking care. Of your father's things. This is good. This is what a son should do. Better later than never.' He repeated this for the benefit of his friend. 'But you rest assured, you sleep easy at night. As I did with your father, I will do with you. I have no intention of, of, of—what?' He looked around at them. 'No intention at all.'

The registrar had given him the record, Mousey said. He had explained to Mousey what was what and what was where.

'These records.' Rafik tapped the map. 'They say what they want.'

'He doesn't understand,' his friend said. 'You give this registrar a little money,' he added slowly, as if he were speaking to a child, 'he'll make the record as you like. Who is he? He's a peasant. What else? You tell him, "Put this plot in this name, that plot in that name," he'll do as you say.' He gestured at different areas on the map. 'The record, you use it instead of this'—he plucked a tissue from the box on the carpet and waved it—'to wipe your nose and mouth. Yes?'

What difference did it make, Rafik said, whose name a plot was in? The land was theirs, and no one could take it from them. 'Sometimes we put a plot in the name of this farmer or that. You know they introduce these rules about how much land a man can hold, so one must find ways around. But you won't bother about all this. I'll send your money every year, as I did with your father, once the farm was under my care. Of course we all want to run away, isn't that so? We all want to be in London at Harrods with all these light-skinned women.' He winked at his friend. 'But then what will happen to this?' He shook a corner of the map. 'It will go to the dogs. And this seat that has been in the family for generations, another will take it like this'—he snapped his fingers—'if I'm not careful.'

Mousey began explaining in that wheedling way he had. This wasn't fair, that wasn't fair. Rafik had done too much, he said—too, too much. To lose a father was a moment that changed one.

'Don't I know?' Rafik said. 'You're a grown man. I was his age.' He waved his hand at the boy. 'I had to do as your father told me. I couldn't do what I wanted. What did I want? I wanted my father's seat. It was my father's. I was entitled. But I was young. When your father was foreign minister, meeting this one and that—Jackie Kennedy, Farah Diba—where was I? Out here, up to my knees, making the money to pay for his elections.'

The TV suddenly turned on, the volume very loud, an ambulance careering across the screen. The remote could not be found. They couldn't hear each other's voices. They pulled up the cushions from the sofa. They looked beneath it too. A teacup fell from the table onto the floor. The friend's son pulled the TV's plug out from the socket. They remained standing. The map had slid half off the table. It curled over the edge.

'When I'd give your father the accounts,' Rafik said, 'he wouldn't want to see. "I have an entry for every farmer," I'd say. "How much seed he took, how much fertiliser, what his yield was, what he gave us." "Don't show it to me," your father would say. "Take it away." He would slap the ledger. He would tear it. "Why?" He would get angry with me. "What is more than family? What is family without trust?"'

Mousey continued talking, twisting one way then the other, wringing his hands like a moneylender. He only wanted the twenty-seven hundred acres that were his, he said.

'This is the reason the society is turning to nothing. Turning to shit. Yours, mine. Everything must be broken into pieces. Your father would weep. My father would weep. You don't understand. You've been away too long.'

Mousey kept on about it. He wasn't going to London, he said. He wasn't going back. He'd stay here and steer the ship himself.

'Absolutely not,' Rafik said finally, standing up. 'I forbid it.'

THREE

AFTER THAT FIRST ENCOUNTER the evening Mousey came to visit, the neighbour boy kept returning to the house as though he were being summoned, sending messages with the servants to Fahad on the landing, and when Fahad didn't come down, he'd come up himself, his heavy footfall echoing up the stairwell, his shadow lengthening on the wall.

He was a thug, the kind of boy Fahad would have gone out of his way to avoid at school, wouldn't have looked in the face, would have hidden from in the music practice rooms in the basement—big hands, broad shoulders, animal eyes that flashed under his heavy brow.

He barely spoke, sat for long periods in absolute silence, scanning the room, splaying his fingers across his knees, the many gathers of his salwar hanging in bunches between his legs. It didn't bother Fahad. The boy could sit where he liked.

For all his swagger, he came and went in a small battered Suzuki, folding into and out of an impossibly tiny front seat. But he and his father clearly held some importance. If Rafik

was in his bedroom, the boy and his father would seek him
out there and if Rafik was on the verandah, some of the
other visitors would stand to clear the seats near the front
for them.

The boy's clothes were pressed and starched, his sturdy
peshawari sandals with their tyre treads for soles polished,
his beard groomed to a point beneath his chin and sharp at
the ends of his moustache. Like the wealthier visitors, he had
a solidness to him.

Why didn't Fahad speak? he asked. People thought he
was strange.

Fahad shrugged. He didn't look up from his book.

Didn't he like it here? the boy asked another time, as
though he were taunting Fahad. What could he want that he
didn't have? He swept his hand towards the ugly walls.

'Things,' Fahad said.

Why didn't he meet people? Why didn't he take his father's big car and travel about? Why didn't he manage the
lands and run the mills? The boy spoke always like he was
shouting, his voice so big it came at Fahad from every direction and even when Fahad kept his head down, he could feel
the boy watching him, his eyes somehow everywhere.

'I HEAR YOU'RE MAKING FRIENDS,' Fahad's mother said
when she called.

'No,' he said. He could hear the radio in the background
playing something classical and imagined knocking it off the
shelf, imagined it cracking in two and his mother holding her
bony face in horror.

She talked about the weather and feeding the ducks at the pond and all the tourists at Harrods. 'You can't escape them anywhere,' she said.

'They're barbarians,' he said, 'the people here.' He'd never go back to the lands. 'It's all he cares about,' he said, meaning his father. 'The lands and the seat, the seat and the lands. It's so base. It's medieval. Isn't there anything else?'

'Make an effort at least,' his mother said. 'Go with him where he goes and maybe you'll see, you'll understand. And'—she paused—'you think he doesn't need it, but he needs it too, a helping hand now and then. He's having a tough old time, even if he won't say. He thinks he's made of stone but he isn't. He isn't at all.'

Fahad made a noise that wasn't a yes or a no. 'He thinks everyone else needs help,' he said. 'Why can't he leave everyone alone?'

IF FAHAD HAD had a room, he could have kept people out, but there was no door to the landing. It was just the top of the stairs. 'Why do you come?' he wanted to ask the boy. 'Don't you have anything to do?' Instead, Fahad stayed on his bed in the corner, with his back to the wall, knees steepled in front of him, shoulders curled over his book. The book was a textbook from the outside, but inside it was the one he'd taken from his mother's shelf. There was a perverse pleasure in reading that while the boy sat there brooding like an ox. He wanted to read aloud. 'She touched her hand to his chest,' he wanted to say. 'She traced the tip of her thumb along his collarbone.' He wanted to make the boy blush. The boy had a strange mouth—dark lips with an exaggerated

Cupid's bow, almost girlish, really the wrong mouth on the wrong face. Sometimes while he watched Fahad, he chewed his lower lip, which was fatter than the upper. Sometimes, his lip spotted with blood.

HE WAS A SAVAGE. But why should Fahad be afraid of him? He wouldn't be. He wasn't. Still he thought of some of the boys at school, of the one who had held a lit match to the back of Fahad's hair. Fahad hadn't known, had wondered why everyone was laughing, and then when he'd felt his neck sting, had smelled that terrible smell, he'd patted it out as though it were nothing at all, the blackened ends streaking his fingers. It was only when he was alone in the bathroom, craning with his back to the mirror over the sink to see what it looked like, that he'd doubled over gasping and coughing and vomited a thin yellow stream into the toilet.

ONCE THE BOY ASKED Fahad what he was reading and when Fahad tilted the cover towards him, the boy nodded and said, 'It's good.' The next time he came, he brought a thin, cheap book, a picture of an earthen pot and large Sindhi script on the cover, 'Ali' written in large wobbly letters on the inside.

'You can learn,' he said. 'I can show you. This is—' And he sounded a letter Fahad had never heard before, smacking the middle of his tongue against the roof of his mouth. 'You do it now,' he said.

Fahad didn't want to—but he tried anyway. 'No, no,' Ali said. He repeated the sound and then Fahad copied him and they did this again and again, percussing a sort of music

together, and at some point despite himself Fahad laughed
and Ali laughed too.

ONE EVENING, Ali came and didn't sit. He stood by the
banister. 'People are here,' he said. 'Your father has called
them. It's good. He wants them to see who the important
man is, who gives them food, who makes their calls for them.'
The single bare bulb that illuminated the landing and stairwell hung from the ceiling behind him so that he was entirely
in shadow. 'The biryani from outside is always better than the
one from home and there are pots and pots of it. Enough for
a thousand at least.'

Fahad refused. And then to test him—why not?—he said,
'If you bring it,' as though Ali were his servant. Ali shook
his head and left. But Fahad listened for his footsteps—and
when he heard them on the stairs, when he saw Ali carrying
a plate piled high, something in his heart gave a little jump,
something shook its fist.

Ali had brought biryani, but also a heap of criss-crossed
charred ribs, a bright yellow dal thick as mashed potato, but-
tery burnished nans scattered with sesame seeds, bombay
aloo. A grain of yellow rice was caught in his beard and Fahad
imagined plucking it out.

He watched Fahad eat as though he had never seen anyone eat before, turning his head one way, then the other, like
a bird almost, like a bird. 'Once,' he began, and then paused a
long while. No, he was embarrassed to say. He hid his lips
behind his fingers and then spoke through them. He'd had a
meal in the dining room downstairs, he said. He'd been too
scared to eat. He didn't know how to use the knife and fork.

'It's nothing difficult,' Fahad said, holding them up, moving them around like jousting sticks.

Ali covered his eyes with his hand.

'Look,' Fahad said. 'Like this.' He showed him how the knife sat in his palm, how he gripped the fork. He stabbed with the fork, sawed in the air with the knife, and then did the same on the paper plate balanced on his knee, which buckled from the pressure, a half-eaten chop sliding off onto the bed.

'This is mine now,' Ali said, grabbing it for himself.

'Only if you eat it with this,' Fahad said. He set the paper plate in front of Ali. He held the knife and fork out to him, each by its handle.

'With this—' Ali waved his hands at Fahad, then ate the chop in a single bite, his lips spread into a broad smile.

When Fahad had finished, Ali said, 'It's like a mela. Your father has done a very good thing. This is what matters the most to people, that they are given food. They forget everything else, that you didn't do this, you didn't do that, if you give them biryani.'

'That's very easy then,' Fahad said.

There was music and dancing and a man telling fortunes, Ali said. Didn't Fahad want to see? People wanted to see him. People were asking. 'You, your family, you're princes here,' he said. 'You're kings.'

THE HALLWAY WAS CROWDED. Ali elbowed his way through, turning to check every now and then that Fahad was behind him, pressing the crowd apart for him to follow.

Smoke hung over the figures in the yard, dipping between

them, curling about their faces. The smell stung Fahad's eyes but it had a lip-licking sweetness too, something that made him hungry again. Along the wall there were giant steel degs—large enough to fit a child—with fires burning under them and men scooping food out with paper plates.

It was loud and Ali had to speak close to Fahad's face, the inside of his mouth bright against the black of his beard. He took Fahad by the wrist from group to group, introducing him to this one and that—peasants in torn shirts who reached to touch Fahad's feet, men with kajol on their eyes and rings on their fingers, a farmer whose lip twisted up into his nostril in a ragged loop, another whose elbows stuck out from his sides like wings. Ali shouted at those who came too near. He tugged them away by their clothes. 'Show some respect,' he said to one man, swelling his chest, squaring his shoulders.

The chatter became louder, punctuated by the clatter of drums, now a kind of chant with something hypnotic in its syncopated rhythms. A full moon appeared suddenly overhead from behind clouds, shining directly upon Fahad as he tripped after Ali, slipping between figures, music thrumming through him, up from the soles of his feet, prickling at the tip of his scalp.

What did anything matter at all, he thought, except the moment you were in, the jostling elbows and knees around him keeping him upright, keeping him from falling.

They tumbled out onto the verandah, Fahad breathless. A man who stood beneath the eaves so that only the lower part of his face was visible asked Fahad to show him his hand. A group gathered round them. He'd tell Fahad's fortune, he said, and had reached for Fahad's fingers, flattened Fahad's palm with his thumb—Fahad laughing, unthinking—tilted it towards the light before he suddenly wrenched it back.

FAHAD ASKED THE SERVANTS about Ali and his father. 'What can we say?' the scruffy bearer said. 'Who will listen to us? These people do what they want. They are no better than bandits.'

His father's manager didn't like them either. 'How much they think of themselves,' he said. 'Who are they to think anything? Barely a hundred acres of land. And they beat their farmers and servants with their own hands even.'

THE STRANGE THING was being together at all. Ali was a brute—the size of him, how he took up space, shoved people aside if they were in his way. With Fahad, though, he became someone else. Once Ali picked up his *Macbeth*, flicked through the pages. 'I can't,' he said, shaking his head blindly at the text, shrugging. What was the point of school? His father had land. They were building a mill. What did he need studies for?

'Is that all there is in the world?' Fahad said.

'What else?'

'Beauty,' Fahad said. 'Art. Theatre. Books.'

'What can you do with these things?' he said. 'You pass the time with them if you have nothing better to do.'

'What do you do with the land? With the mill?'

'You make money.'

'And with the money?'

'Whatever you want,' Ali said. 'With money you are free.'

'And what would you do with freedom?'

He sighed and frowned. 'Why think of it now?' he said.

But he'd teach Fahad how to hunt, he said after a moment. 'That's a thing to learn.'

What great skill was it for a man with a gun to shoot an animal? Fahad wanted to know. 'Fight with your hands, if you're so strong,' he wanted to say, and then imagined, for some reason, an unexpected thrill thrumming through him, the two of them grappling, tumbling across the dusty carpet, their hands gripping each other.

WHAT DID HIS FATHER think of it all? He should have been happy but he was preoccupied—touring the lands sometimes twice a day, morning and just before Maghrib in the evening. There had been an altercation with the registrar—his father dragging the man out of the house by his long, white beard, all the other visitors watching from a safe distance. 'You should be in the fields with the rest of your family, you dog,' he said. 'It was my father, my father, *my father* who gave you a salary, who gave you a job.'

FAHAD COMPLAINED ABOUT the food at the house to Ali. 'You live in a palace,' Ali said, 'but your servants are no good. They do as they like. Nobody tells them what to do.'

It wasn't a palace, more like a prison, a fortress—its high, narrow windows, its crenellated walls, its dark passageways.

'I know what puts a smile on your face,' Ali said.

And Fahad for some reason blushed.

The best ice cream in the district. Ali would take him. People came from all over for the sundaes at the Greenland Hotel. They had their own buffalo so the milk was fresh and full of cream.

He wouldn't eat outside the house, Fahad said. 'Everything is so dirty here.' But he'd come for the ride.

ALI LOOKED ABSURD in his Suzuki—shoulders pressed against the steering wheel, knees halfway up his chest. They drove through the avenue of neem trees that led from the house to the road, through the arch at the end of it.

The sun was low in the sky. The sky was copper. Fahad wound down the window, stuck his elbow out, the air currents whipping at his collar. 'It's freedom to be leaving.' He laughed. 'Anything can happen.'

They left the lands behind them. The sky dimmed to a silvery twilight—a magical glow. He wanted to sing, he wanted to dance.

Ali talked about Fahad's father, that Ali was too scared to speak in front of him, that he wanted to but when he opened his mouth no words came out.

'You look like a lion but you're a mouse,' Fahad said—and poked him in the ribs.

The tall grass in the fields rippled and the trees at the edges looked like figures waving. The breeze outside was hot and worried a plastic Koran that dangled from Ali's rearview mirror.

'Why Karachi when you can have this?' Ali said. 'You can walk from your house for days and you'll be only on your own land.' At the police chowki by the town's limits, a policeman waved his baton at them to stop. He twisted the points at the end of his moustache.

'You bastard, what will you take from us?' Ali called out, weaving round him, waving with the back of his hand.

'Here you can do what you want,' Ali continued. They rattled through ditches and divots past a series of mills, the chimneys smoking, the yards stacked with grain. 'If he had seen who was in the car with me, he would have been ashamed he had tried to stop us.'

From here the shops and stalls began, the strange music of the place: a mechanic chiming a wrench against the wheel of a tractor, children calling after a pair of goats skipping across the street, a fruit seller singing his wares.

'You haven't been to the cinema,' Ali said, wobbling his head in a funny way. 'I'll take you. Shall I? They show special movies.' He winked.

'We'll go every day,' Fahad said, surprising himself, and then they both laughed.

Ali pulled up by the side of the road, where waiters with trays were lolling about, smacking the trays against their legs. Ali signalled at one of them.

'Not for me,' Fahad said, as Ali gave instructions from the car to the man, holding up two thick fingers. 'I won't.'

It was like a dance, the movement outside, figures in that pleasant half-light slipping between each other, turning around, dipping out of sight. And the scene behind them seemed flat as a stage set—the white walls of the hotel, the red canopy of a stall selling pakoras, the green awning of a parked rickshaw.

A beggar girl sprung up from beside the rickshaw, darted

towards Fahad's window. She tapped the glass and held her fingers to her mouth. Her hair was light and hung in ragged ropes around her face. There was a crust at the corners of her lips and around her nose. She was maybe six or seven or eight or nine or fifteen or twenty or a hundred.

The waiter reappeared with two tall glasses of ice cream and brightly coloured crushed ice—in swirls of blue, orange, and green. Fahad shook his head but took the glass Ali handed him.

'You're so delicate?' Ali shovelled a spoonful into his mouth, strands of vermicelli hanging from the spoon and now from his lips. 'One bite and you'll break?' Fahad held the glass between his thighs.

The girl tapped on the window again, saying something inaudible, repeating it and pointing at her mouth. 'No,' Fahad said, and shook his hand. 'She won't go away.'

Ali laughed. 'Just tell her,' he said.

The ice cream glass had a flared rim so that as the ice cream melted, it wobbled perilously at the edges. He felt the girl watching him and without turning waved at her to leave. The blurry reflection in the windscreen was probably her.

A car slid up alongside Ali's car, music playing and shadows moving. Ali nudged Fahad—it was Mousey's jeep. Inside, there was a man he didn't recognise and, in the driver's seat, Mousey.

'The servant should be driving,' Ali said.

'Is he a servant?' Fahad said—the man had a sort of professional neatness about him. He could have been a bank teller. Even an actor.

'It's his manager.'

From where he sat, Fahad could see more of Mousey's

face than his manager's. Mousey was laughing. Mousey was talking. Mousey was waving his hands as he talked.

'You should say something,' Ali said. 'What he has done is very bad. He has made your father look dishonest. He has told people your father is using his power to bully him, to keep from him what is his, what his father left him. He has told people the seat is his. That it was his father's before him.'

'Father, father, father,' Fahad said. 'No more fathers. A world without fathers.'

'They say your father has begged him on his knees,' Ali continued. 'I don't believe it. That he says it is his turn now and after him Mousey may have his turn. Why is he afraid? No man should want a thing so much.'

The man leaned in towards Mousey, and Mousey pushed him away.

'It's like they're friends,' Fahad said. 'Like they're boys. Like they're playing.'

The man touched the tip of his thumb to Mousey's face, to the notch between Mousey's lip and his chin.

Fahad and Ali turned sharply away.

'People say things about him,' Ali said.

'What things?'

'He's your uncle. I won't say.'

'He's a bastard,' Fahad said. 'What things?'

'That his manager sleeps inside his house.'

Where exactly did he sleep, Fahad wanted to know. What exactly did Ali mean. He wanted to ask him that. He wanted to challenge him to say more. And who do you think you are, anyway, he wanted to say, to speak like that about my family.

Fahad ate a spoonful of ice cream only so that it wouldn't drip. It was too sweet and there were chips of ice in it. There were nuts and shards of a kind of brittle. The translucent vermicelli looped round his spoon, streaked with the coloured syrups swirled through the dish. It wasn't unpleasant but something in it had a medicinal bitterness, something coated the inside of his mouth with fur.

That beggar girl was still at the window. She thudded her fist against it and when he looked, when he gestured at her again to move, when he put his hands together as though he were praying and said, though she couldn't hear, though she couldn't understand, 'Please just go somewhere else,' she squashed her face against the pane, flattening her nose, spreading her lips apart to show her gums, smearing the glass.

'Look,' Fahad said. 'Look at what she's done.' He felt an ugly pressure on his brow, felt his eyes prickle.

Ali climbed out of the car, his half-empty glass in his fist. The girl hurried away now, round the side of the stall.

'She's gone, it's alright,' Fahad said.

But Ali caught up with her. He grabbed her by the shirt. She squalled like a cat and he slapped her across the back of her head, shoved her so that she fell, knocking her cheek against a concrete ledge.

'Your ways,' Ali said when he'd returned to the car, handing the glass to the waiter, wiping his hands on a handful of napkins the waiter had brought, tossing them out onto the road, 'they're alright for you people. But here there must be something else.'

Mousey was gone. Had he seen them? Fahad wondered afterwards. What was there to see anyway?

FOUR

FAHAD'S FATHER GAVE him a gun. 'Are you becoming a man?' he said. It was in a long leather briefcase. His father set it upon his bed. He flicked on his desk lamp and pivoted the beam onto the case. He snapped the locks open. There was a long black barrel in dull metal, a stock of nut-coloured wood, a sight, and several steel rods, each slotted into green baize lining.

A friend had given it, his father said. He'd never even put it together. 'A man who needs a gun, what power does he have?' his father said. 'Only as much as the gun.' He shut the case, squeezed the locks closed.

He sat the case on its edge, handed it to Fahad. He seemed to want to say more, keeping hold of its handle even as Fahad slipped his fingers under it. The lamplight glowed upon his face and a lock of hair fell across his forehead. 'This much I know,' he said finally.

Fahad lugged the case upstairs and slid it under his bed.

———

HE SHOWED IT to Ali. 'I don't want to hunt,' he said. 'But shouldn't I know how it works?'

'This is too old,' Ali said, running the tip of his thumb along the barrel. 'Antique. That's why you like it. Just to look. But I have many. I'll show you.'

Was it even just knowing that it was there under the bed that made Fahad different, made him send his dinner back once when it was no good, made him tell a visitor he'd marry when he damn well wanted and not when anyone told him, made him shout at the bearer for moving his books, at the sweeper for leaving a trail of lint across the floor?

LATER IN THE WEEK, Ali collected Fahad from the house, sounding his horn just as the bearer was sliding the bolt up on the front door. It was an unfamiliar sight—Fahad had never imagined the house shut up at all. Was he going so late, the bearer asked, his fingers pinching the bolt but not yet lowering it.

He was, Fahad said, and, pushing the man out of the way, lowered it himself.

Ali's car was idling outside, in a pool of very dim light. Overhead, the moon was fine as a sickle. A cloud passed across it.

They drove in silence—Ali speeding and the air currents through the windows tearing at their hair and clothes. The headlamps were so faint, it seemed as though they were racing endlessly into nothing. It made Fahad feel like he was falling. He steadied himself against the dashboard, talking mindlessly about things—the call his father had received from the finance minister, the crow that had dropped a scrap of roti onto the cook's head, the temple on the lands that he wanted to see for himself, they should just knock the damn thing down, his father was too easy on these people. Something darted into the road, Ali swerved and braked, the brakes screaming, a thud and another thud under the car—a thud and another thud.

The car had stopped.

'It was nothing,' Ali said. 'An animal.' His knuckles gleamed like pebbles against the steering wheel. 'A dog maybe.'

The road behind them had disappeared into the dark. Ali reversed, swinging to one side then correcting himself, then swinging the other way. 'There.' The shape in the road was no bigger than a child, hunched over as if in prayer.

'What is it?' Fahad said—something shaking through him, making his voice shake too.

'It's nothing,' Ali said.

'Look—' Fahad said. Had it moved? Was it moving? Their breaths became short together.

'No,' Ali said, but then drove very slowly alongside, peering out of his open window. 'A dog,' he said. 'Only a dog.'

They continued along—and every time they drove over a bump, or through a ditch, thud, thud, Fahad heard it again, the second sound always a little softer than the first, like a pair of heartbeats.

'It happens all the time,' Ali said. 'You see them on the side of the road.' After a moment, he added, 'Why did it cross? The road is empty. There's no one else. It could have gone before or after. There's no one else.'

The expression on his face made him unfamiliar, his mouth twisted under his moustache, his eyes dark lines, or perhaps the strange glow from the headlights distorted everything. 'His grandfather was shot by his own farmer,' his father's manager had said of Ali, 'the man was so cruel.'

Why was it so far? Why had Ali told him not to bring his own gun? Why did the road never end?

Then Ali turned so sharply, at such high speed, that the rear of the car swung out to the side. 'I didn't see the way,' he said, flicking his lights to full beam onto a dirt track, where the trees were so close it seemed the track was only wide enough to travel on foot—but he urged the car on, the tyres spitting up stones that ricocheted off the chassis, the branches scraping against the doors and clawing though the windows, till Fahad wound his up.

'Is this the way?' Fahad said. 'It's a forest.' He looped his fingers round the handle of his door—but where was he going to go?

It was nothing, he told himself. It was Ali. He wasn't a stranger. 'You didn't teach me the language,' he said, holding on to that memory, trying to laugh. He sounded the letter Ali had tried to teach him to say. 'Is that right?' he said. He sounded it again and again after that. 'Is that how you say it? Like that?'

'They should be here,' Ali said. 'Just ahead.'

Who were 'they'? A shadow crept across the dashboard.

'Who?' Fahad said.

Suddenly, they were in a clearing. A pickup truck flashed bright lights and Fahad imagined a bundle like the one they'd seen on the road tossed into the back. Ali leaned far out of his window and called out towards the truck. It revved its engine. Then it sped ahead and they rattled after it.

Fahad imagined the bundle tumbling around the back of the truck. Imagined a child's arm uncurling from it.

'I'll take you to my house later,' Ali said.

He didn't know him at all, Fahad thought. He didn't.

The track became rockier, the tyres raced, and dust clouded up around them. They skidded forward and the dust remained on the windows and windscreen, casting a veil over everything outside.

'How late is it?' Fahad asked. Why was it so late?

Ali stopped the car. The truck had parked nearby and shone its bright lights at a low wall.

Men poured out of the truck. They set up a table, spread a cloth over it, and huddled round it, busy at some work. Mingling with their rough voices were jungle sounds—the saw of crickets, birds shrieking, branches breaking as though something were moving insistently closer.

Ali put his hand on Fahad's back and pushed him towards the table. 'Now,' he said, 'you will understand.'

There were guns of various shapes—short and squat, long and narrow, long and broad. Some had straps thick as belts folded against them. Ali stopped in front of a rifle that looked a little like the one Fahad's father had given him. He hooked his finger behind the trigger and swung it off the table. Fahad's heart jolted in his chest. Ali propped the gun on his shoulder, took aim, and, as he fired towards the wall, Fahad stumbled backwards, feeling for the car, wondering wildly if the key were in the ignition, if he could find the way home.

Birds had startled from the field and hung in the sky for a moment as though suspended. A sound chimed, then a zing like flint sparking.

There were bottles and canisters along the top. Ali fired again and now one of them shattered, the glass exploding like a firework.

'You try,' he said to Fahad, without looking round, then fired once more. The moon had reappeared, its sickle curving as if from the tip of Ali's barrel.

He slid the gun off his shoulder and turned back. He shouted and one of the men took a smaller gun—a revolver—from the table and handed it to Fahad. It was heavier than Fahad had expected—unreasonably heavy for something so small—and the muscles in his arm strained as he extended it.

'No, no,' Ali said, pushing Fahad's wrist to lower the gun. 'Not like this.' Then, gripping Fahad by his shoulders, Ali positioned him so that he was at the place Ali had been standing. He squared Fahad's hips. 'Now,' he said.

Fahad raised his arm again. The wall seemed impossibly far away all of a sudden, the objects on it as tiny as the birds that had been only moments ago overhead.

'Choose one,' Ali said—and Fahad chose a canister like the one kept in the car with sweets.

The field ahead sloped downwards so that it seemed from here that the wall was a cliff edge, that he was facing the sky and the sky was enormous. He became very still and around him became very still. He wasn't frightened anymore. Or he was and he wasn't at the same time.

He squeezed the trigger and the gun fired, jolting his arm up, knocking him backwards against Ali, who steadied him. 'It's very strong,' Ali said. 'Next time like this.' He extended his arm alongside Fahad's, pressed Fahad's legs apart with his own, straightened Fahad's foot with his foot. He positioned Fahad's wrist. Ali's body was sturdy as the trunk of a tree and when Fahad fired again, this time he lurched against Ali but remained in the same stance. 'Again,' Ali said. 'Whatever happens you look at the thing you want. Are you looking?'

He was. Though he had the sensation he was looking at a bottle on the wall and looking at himself looking. He was himself and separate from himself, standing and watching himself stand, thinking and watching himself think. He fired again, but this time he stood fast, digging his heels in, and the force of the blast juddered through him, from his skull down his spine, his hips down his legs to the soles of his feet and into the ground as though he were made of the same stuff as the gun in his hand, as though the gun were made of the same stuff as the earth and the sound shook through his chest like his own voice.

FIVE

A SORT OF MADNESS took hold of Rafik: a delirium that was sometimes rage, sometimes crazed abandon. 'What's happened?' Soraya said, when he called. 'Are you alright? Talking and talking like I'm your buddy and not your wife.'

He talked about the boy, that he'd made a friend, that he went out and about, to the town in the evenings, to eat. 'Only a month with me and I'm setting him straight,' he said.

She wanted to know what the friend was like.

'He's an ordinary sort. Like any other. Local toughie. He's teaching Fahad to shoot.'

She made a fuss about that. There were accidents. People got hurt. She wanted him to promise the boy wouldn't do it again. She insisted. 'You go to the jungle and you turn into beasts.'

'This is the difference,' he said. 'Here we are the ones with guns.' He talked about Mousey too, that he'd decided not to go back to London, that he had all sorts of ideas, 'all very strange.' He did not say that Mousey wanted his lands back.

He did not mention the turban binding ceremony that had taken place in secret a few nights earlier. 'He comes after thirty years, after forty. Where was he when his father was dying? Where was he when I was alone looking after all this? When I had to borrow money because his father wouldn't give it? When I didn't sleep day or night from worry?'

'The snake,' Soraya said. 'The rat. Don't trust him as far as you can throw him. But he's a tiny one, you could throw him a mile.'

There was a time she'd been fond of Mousey. Mousey this, Mousey that. The flat he had in Cadogan Gardens, the cruise he took down the Nile. 'You used to like him,' he said.

'Who?' she said. And he wished for a moment he could feel the back of her hand against his brow.

'He's trying all these new ways,' he said, his face becoming hot, his chest becoming tight. 'Spending millions and millions, they say. Bringing seed and new equipment from China. Sold everything he had. If it doesn't work, then he'll be in a jam. He'll have to go back, the bastard. And it won't work. He doesn't know. His father sat on his bloody ass all day and waited for me to send him his money, his share from the lands. Receiving visitors as minister of this, minister of that. It was my father who made the family's name.'

'You think everyone is your disciple,' she said. 'More the fool you.' What would Mousey even do there, she said, a man like him.

'And you?' he said. 'You're happy? Spending my money?'

'Go to hell,' she said. 'Without me you'd be in the jungle still.'

———

THE TURBAN BINDING was a ceremony to appoint the chief of the tribe. Someone had put Mousey up to it, of course. Mousey didn't know about these things. Someone would have said, 'You do it before Rafik does. After all, it was your father. You're the son. The son is the heir.' It was stupidness. It was troublemaking. And just like Mousey to do a thing behind the back rather than to the face. What did it matter at all? Let him call himself the chief of goddamn Timbuktu if he wanted. It didn't mean they'd give him their votes. It didn't mean he'd win the seat if he tried for it. And this lot here who were at Rafik's house one day, eating the food at his table, having him call this official or that for favours, they were at Mousey's the next day. They turned whichever way the wind blew. He'd give each and every one a slap with his fist the next time he saw them. He'd knock them to Timbuktu, where they could be happy with Mousey.

WHEN THEY DROVE around the lands, Rafik showed Fahad what a mess Mousey was making of things. 'It may look fuller, but this Chinese seed, you can't reuse it. Each year you have to buy it again. And see how late this crop is. Ours is already four feet high, his barely a foot.' Mousey's crop had a deeper colour and a lushness to it—but let the time for the harvest come, then they'd see.

The boy had learnt to drive—so he wouldn't have to sit in the back with the manager and others—but stopped and started, used a gear too low or too high. 'Third,' Rafik said, 'if you're going so fast. No, don't slow down. Just go up a gear.' He shook the gear stick. The boy slowed down wherever water had spilled across the track, wherever there were ditches. 'Keep going, it's fine. Don't turn, don't turn. Just keep it straight. If it's sliding just keep going. No, it won't get stuck.' But now it did. 'Now it won't help to keep the tyres turning. It will make it worse. Just stop. Stop. Turn off the engine.'

It was so muddy outside they had to wait for farmers to be found in a nearby village to carry them out of the jeep onto higher land and then, knee-deep in the stuff, the farmers lifted the jeep out of the muck.

'Why don't you keep the wheel straight?' he told the boy. 'Don't turn this way and that way, like something that doesn't know where it's going. Like this always—' And he dashed his hand like a blade through the air.

It was too muddy, the boy said. 'They should fix it—the road.' And then when they were back in the car Fahad told the manager as much. 'You keep the roads like this so we can't use them. Then we can't see the work you aren't doing. You're all thieves.'

He kept returning to the site of the temple, circling around that field as though he were looking for something.

'What are you doing?' Rafik said. 'We've been this way. We've seen this. Go on.' He gestured towards the smoke spiralling from the chimney of the rice mill. But the boy came back to the temple again.

'I want to look,' he said. 'From here it doesn't look like there's anything, just the trees.'

His manager was a nervous sort, telling the boy it wasn't a good idea, telling him to leave it alone.

'If you want to see, then see,' Rafik said. 'But get it over with.'

This saint was a wicked woman, the manager said. She

hung from the branches of trees to frighten people passing underneath. They said women who wanted children went to her, but women who didn't want them went too.

'Whatever it is, you decide, but hurry up,' Rafik said. The boy parked the car where the path began that led through the field to the temple. The paddy was so high, so verdant, that the boy disappeared into it. 'You're letting him go alone?' Rafik told the manager. 'Go.'

HE'D REMEMBERED A THING that had happened when they were boys, he and Mousey. At night, Rafik didn't sleep so well now, a feverish rage stirring him in the hours before Fajr, prickling at the ends of his fingertips, at the top of his scalp. Sometimes he'd dream standing up in his dressing room on the way to or from the bathroom. Those waking dreams were unlike sleeping dreams—these were closer to thoughts or desires or memories, illuminating some further recess of his mind as though some things could only be seen in half-light.

He'd remembered in one of those dreams. Mousey had had a friend a year or two younger than him—they were always together at the gates or by the tuck shop, always sitting close and whispering. It wasn't such a queer thing but people talked and made up stories and a name for Mousey. What had they called him? It had stuck, so that even people who didn't know him so well shouted that name out in class or assembly. They were being silly, that was all. And Mousey, true to form, said nothing. But one day, a group of them called out to him as he was crossing the quad, using that name—whatever it had been. Mousey had calmly walked over towards the ring-leader, lifted the bottle of cola he was holding, and smashed

it into the side of the boy's head. The boy didn't move away
or duck. The blow knocked him to the ground, where he
lay with a raw wound the size of a fist just above his ear,
his hair matted with blood. Mousey stood there, the neck of
the bottle still in his hand, jagged at the edges. When he remembered it, Rafik had felt his face and the back of his neck
growing hot with a strange kind of thrill and terror; Mousey's
rage and the rage of the boy he had struck.

That was why his father and Mumtaz had sent Mousey to
London. There'd have been trouble otherwise. Rafik hadn't
thought about it in years—so long that he'd forgotten entirely what had prompted Mousey to leave in the first place
but now he couldn't unremember it, the stage set across
which everything played.

Fahad was scrambling up the verge, with the manager behind him. 'There is a temple,' he said. 'Not a temple but a
tomb. But we saw something much better. You won't believe
it. Guess.'

'You took a long time,' Rafik said. 'Come on.'

Fahad clambered back into the car.

'I said we shouldn't,' the manager said, his collar streaked
with dirt. 'It wasn't right. These people—they don't like being disturbed. They're very powerful. They can do many
things.'

'There are no people,' Fahad said, starting the car with a
jerk. 'There was a tomb and lots of little tombs around it—
like graves for children.'

'Okay, okay,' Rafik said. 'Now you go back along the canal
road.'

'But I heard a noise. Behind a bush. He saw it.' Fahad
tipped his head towards the manager in the back. 'A cat, but

huge.' He spread his arms wide, leaving the wheel unattended for a moment, the car swinging to the left.

'What are you doing?' Rafik said, as he righted it.

'As big as a cow. No, maybe smaller. Maybe a dog. With ears like this.' He gestured with his fingers at the sides of his head. They climbed up onto the canal bank. 'But its mouth was covered in blood. It had killed something. Or something had bitten it. A snake, maybe.'

'What else could it have been but a snake?' the manager said.

'You're not listening,' Fahad said.

'You focus on the way,' Rafik said. 'I'm listening. A snake.'

'But there were babies, little cats hiding behind. It was a mother,' Fahad said.

'Very good,' Rafik said.

'You said there weren't snakes here,' Fahad said.

'There are,' Rafik said. 'Of course there are. This was all jungle.'

Mousey had begged Rafik to convince his father, to convince Mumtaz Chacha. He hadn't wanted to leave. But it was the right thing. He'd sent letters from London to Rafik, strange letters, funny drawings of boys and other things—Rafik didn't want to think of it. Mumtaz Chacha had never been so fond of Mousey, always telling him, 'Look at Rafik. You should be like he is. You should do what he does.' But then in recent years, he'd talked of Mousey sometimes, remembered him in a way that wasn't true at all, boasted about the things he'd done. 'He was clever to go,' he'd say sometimes. 'Look at us here.' And then in those last weeks, he'd asked for him often. 'Bring the boy,' he'd said. 'Where's the boy? You're not the boy. Bring him, bring him.' He'd get angry. He'd shout at people. He'd knock things off his bedside table, smash a glass. 'Tell the boy, you're not telling him. If he knew, he'd be here.' Better when he's out of his misery, Rafik thought at times like that.

And Rafik had sent messages to Mousey right from the start, that his father wasn't well, that he didn't have much time.

How much time, Mousey wanted to know.

Who could answer that but God?

Should he come now, Mousey wanted to know. He'd get the next flight if he had to.

'Who can say,' Rafik had said, and in the end Mousey had come too late. Why did you come at all, Rafik wanted to ask him.

'Why did I come?' Fahad said.

'What?' Rafik said.

'You told me to.'

'Yes, yes,' Rafik said. 'You go on with your story.'

Fahad frowned at him. After a moment, glancing again at Rafik, glancing in the rearview mirror, he continued about the temple, that the blood was fresh on the animal's muzzle, that whatever it was had just happened, perhaps even while they were there walking about in that place—no, they'd have heard something.

The canal surged with water still, the water churning at the banks, and the boy asked about that now. How long did the water come for, and where did it come from, and who said when it would come and when it wouldn't and what happened if it didn't come.

'How much work it is,' Rafik explained. 'Sometimes it doesn't come. Then I must speak to this one and that, in the Irrigation Department, in the Ministry, and time is ticking.

The season doesn't wait. The crop doesn't wait. When paddy needs water, it must have it or it dies. In days, in a week even. The year's money gone.' He told the boy to stop where the bank was higher and he showed him the network of watercourses that branched out like arteries from the canal across the lands. 'It's all a system,' he said. 'With gates to let the water go or stop. And gravity does the rest.'

The boy was looking again for the temple. 'There it is,' he said. 'It looks like nothing from here. Smaller than a house.'

'All of this, as far as you can see,' Rafik told him. 'Hills and trees before. You wouldn't recognise it. All of it ours. All of this I did.' He held his hands out—as if he had dug the dirt himself—and it seemed that they were trembling.

But what was Mousey's, the boy wanted to know. And was he going to take the seat as well?

'He'll this, he'll that,' Rafik said. 'He'll get his dues.'

IN THE EVENING, he sent for the boy. 'Sit,' he said. The newspapers didn't reach Abad till the late afternoon and Rafik read them after Maghrib, on the carpet between the two narrow beds in his room, his back against a cushion against the bedside table, the desk lamp on the table pivoted over him. But now he couldn't read for some reason, the print so small it dizzied him, the pages so delicate they tore.

'I was going to go,' Fahad said. 'With my friend.'

'It's good you have friends.'

He hovered by the door.

'Go, go,' Rafik said.

The boy went and then returned. 'I'll go another day,' he said. He'd brought a book and sat, his feet tucked under him on the sofa, the way his mother sat sometimes. 'Carbon copy of the mother,' Rafik said. 'She's a decent woman. A man needs that. Or where will he get comfort?'

The boy turned the pages of his book. The clock ticked loudly.

'He's a good friend?' Rafik said.

'Ali?' The boy shrugged. 'He's okay.'

'Is it different here from there?' It was easier somehow like this, the papers between them like a purdah.

'Not really,' the boy said. Then, 'It feels different.' Ali had ideas, he said. Why didn't they run the rice mill themselves instead of leasing it out? 'We could make millions.'

'We'll think about it,' Rafik said. 'You have to be here for these things. Otherwise they steal. You come back in a month or two and everything is gone. "There were insects," they'll say. Or, "The buyer didn't pay," or some excuse.'

The bearer appeared in the doorway to announce a visitor. 'Tell him I'm resting,' Rafik said, and sent him away.

'Not so many people are coming now,' the boy said.

'They see which way the wind blows,' Rafik said. 'One day here, the next there, if they think he will give money or importance, if they think he'll have a position they can benefit from.'

They sat awhile then, Rafik looking at the cartoons on the back, at the empty squares of the crossword.

'I'll tell you one thing,' he said. 'So many years people said after I married, "When will you have children, when will you have children." Here they concern themselves with all this.' The boy continued looking at his book but inclined his head towards Rafik. 'We saw this doctor and that, experts in London even. They said there's no problem. Everything down there is a-okay. Then it happened just like that. Your mother told me she was expecting. Everyone said, inshallah it will be a boy, God will give you a son.' He tossed the paper to one side and felt on his bed for the city supplement. Finding it, he unfolded it across his knees, flapped it open. 'But in my head for some reason, I thought of a girl, kept thinking I wanted that even, it was what I imagined. I didn't say it to anyone. A man should want a son. Even when you were born, they called to tell me. I heard them say, "It's a daughter." Of course they didn't say it but I was so sure, I had made up my mind, that was what I heard. Then everyone kept saying, "Mubarak, it's a boy." And look now. It's a funny thing.' The story had surprised him, that he'd told it at all of course, but first, that he'd even thought of it. It was as though the stories in his head had been dug up like ruins and now wherever he went in his mind, he stumbled across them.

'It's good,' he added. 'It couldn't be better. A daughter couldn't come here with me, couldn't help.'

'I guess,' the boy said.

The TV was on and again the volume became impossibly high, the siren of an ambulance shrieking, the camera panning across shrouded bodies by the side of the road. The boy tossed up the cushions on the sofa searching for the remote. There was a shot now of bloody bandages wrapped around a face, stains where the eyes might be. The boy shouted for the bearer, who came running in, plucked the remote up from between Rafik's feet, turned the TV off.

Then, Rafik said, 'So what should I do about this one, the Other Sir, as they call him? Whose Sir he is, I don't know.'

'It's like he's challenging you,' the boy said. 'And if you don't do something . . .' He trailed off.

'What I want to do,' Rafik said, 'is this—' And he rubbed
his thumb against an imaginary window like he was squashing an insect. He told him the story about Mousey that he'd
remembered and, retelling it, it seemed that the story was
telling Rafik something.

'But why,' the boy began, and then fell silent. After a
while Rafik wondered, had he gone up to his room? Always
getting up and going, never sitting still. But when Rafik lowered his paper the boy was still there, frowning at the wall,
his fist at his mouth. He shook his head. Finally, he said, 'Ali
says, "You think you have the upper hand, because you have
the gun, but you're in the animal's home, in the forest or the
jungle. It has many things and all you have is the gun."'

'I'm glad you have a friend,' Rafik said. Had he said that
already? 'Your mother doesn't want you doing all this with
guns. She worries.'

'I'm only learning,' the boy said. 'Learning can't be bad.'

A cat shrieked outside the window followed by another—
they shrieked at each other, becoming increasingly frenzied,
then voices, the slap of water on stone, a last squall, and
silence.

'I don't know why,' Rafik said, 'I keep waking in the night,
three on the dot. Sometimes one minute before, sometimes
one minute after.'

Fahad closed his book and set it on the table. He came
over to the bed, sat on the edge. After a moment he put his
hand on Rafik's shoulder and squeezed it.

SIX

THE IDEA CAME to Rafik while he was praying. He had not always prayed so regularly but recently he had found himself needing those moments of quiet obeisance. The words of the prayer moved across his lips as he bowed, knelt, touched his forehead to the ground. I am your servant, he said. I am your servant. And the mat was a raft and his life was the water and when he prostrated himself for the last time, when he raised his head and opened his eyes, the wetness on his lashes made the lights in the room sparkle like jewels.

It was the Isha prayer. The bearer was unloading the dinner tray onto the low table by the sofa when Rafik told him to ready the car. 'You're going somewhere?' the man said.

'Why would I take the car unless I was going somewhere?'

THE SERVANTS HAD SETTLED down in their quarters for the evening but at his summons, they gathered on the porch, pulling their shirts on and unrumpling their hair, the driver fixing the straps on his sandals.

'Is there a wedding this evening?' his manager asked. 'Is there a condolence?'

There was not, Rafik said. These people must know everything.

He told the manager to go ahead on his motorcycle, to round up twenty or thirty farmers, to bring them to a particular place on the canal bank with jute sacks and shovels.

'It's late,' the manager said. 'People will be resting. There are no lights. How will they see?'

'You heard me, or you didn't?' Rafik said.

The driver drove slowly, bent over the steering wheel. 'You're an old man,' Rafik said.

'At this time, I don't see so well,' the driver said, worrying his fingers through his beard. Stones crunched under the tyres. The moon made a streak of silver like a spine down the centre of the canal. 'I taught you to drive on my knee,' the old man said. 'You remember your father's old Ford. You would complain how hot the seats were, how they stuck to your legs when you sat.' Some creature scuttled across the track— a lizard perhaps. 'For your father also,' he said, 'it wasn't so simple. Your grandfather favoured him. Your uncle wasn't happy. But your father was the elder.'

'It was a Plymouth,' Rafik said. 'The Ford came after.'

'It happens in every family,' the driver continued.

'Is this every family?' Rafik said.

About halfway down the canal, Rafik instructed him to stop. Farmers had gathered here with sticks and guns and shovels, his manager's motorcycle, parked at an angle under a tree, directing the dim beam from its headlamp low into the sky.

Rafik told them what he wanted them to do. 'Yes?' the

manager said—he paused a moment and then, when Rafik didn't explain further, turned his attention to the farmers who had begun shovelling soil from a mound by the bank into the bags, the blades ringing against the earth.

A friend had said to him, 'To do nothing is weakness.'

Another had said, 'Restraint—that takes strength, that takes power. Now you are the elder and you cannot think of what you want. You must think of what is correct, what is right.'

Others had said, 'You've been slow to act.' Others had said, 'It was his father, it's his due.' Others had said, 'People don't recognise you. Your hand is so light. Is there no vigour left in it?'

Twenty bags had been filled and stacked in a pyramid along the verge. The beam from the motorcycle guttered and then went out.

He wanted them to carry the sacks into the canal, to lay them like bricks across it. 'But it will stop the water,' his manager said.

'Idiot,' Rafik said. 'Now you're using this.' And he knocked the knuckle of his thumb against his temple.

'This land will have no water,' his manager said. 'This crop the Other Sir has planted needs water very much. Its season is later than ours.'

'How many Sirs do you have?' Rafik said. 'Do you have another father?'

The man bowed his head, his eyes flickering towards the farmers watching. 'The canal will overflow its banks,' he said after a moment.

'Didn't I tell you to open all these watercourses that come before? Empty the water out into the wasteland. Do

what you have to, but the water will not go further than this.'
He marked the point with his foot.

The farmers carried the sacks into the canal, battling the current, the water up to their necks. A sack twisted loose and swam downstream, its mouth flaring, the earth spilling out onto the surf in thick clods. He shouted at them to hold each sack in place, to stand on the far side of the wall they were building—and to those on the bank, to tie the bags tighter.

More bags had to be filled—the canal was so deep and wide. The men gasped as they swung the sacks onto their backs and drew short sharp breaths as they descended into the water. The water roared and thudded as the dam came up, shrieked and moaned as it sluiced across the sacks. But once the dam was complete, the water quietened to a whisper, to a murmur.

Rafik ordered two of the men to watch over the canal with their guns and dismissed the rest. 'If this goes'—he indicated the dam—'then you go too. I'll flatten your homes with the Russian tractor.'

Beyond the dam, there was a shallow sludge in the canal, barely a few inches deep, a flotsam of twigs and branches, leaves, stones, plastic bags, and sweet wrappers, a twist of tinfoil. A tiny dirt-coloured bird hopped through the mud, pecking at a spot here, at one there. The fields ahead were still as death. The night sky seemed to be paling. A hot breeze tugged at his sleeve, unloosed a lock of hair across his forehead. Rafik saw himself standing there alone as if from above.

HE WOKE SUDDENLY to find his breakfast tray upon the table, footsteps outside his window, outside his door. He was jovial with the bearer though his tea was cold, though his toast was dry. 'You entertain girls here when I'm away?' he said. 'That's what they tell me, you rascal.'

Outside, Mousey's farmers had gathered and fell at his feet, women amongst them too. They cried and tore their hair and tugged at his clothes and made their faces wretched.

'We are your children,' they said. 'There is God and then you.'

'You have another Sir,' he said. 'Why are you here? Ask him to help you.'

'You are punishing us,' they said. 'We are your children and you are punishing us.'

He shook them off. 'Who shall I punish then,' he said, 'if not my children?' He went to see the dam, see that it held still.

It did, though farmers had gathered here too—arguing, shoving, and jostling. One of them wouldn't get out of the way and Rafik hit him across the face. Mousey's crop drooped in the fields beyond the dam, the stalks bowing their tips towards him.

'Have some mercy,' they said. 'How will we eat? How will we feed our children and our cattle?'

'The Other Sir,' Rafik said. 'The Other Sir will give all the answers you want.'

SEVEN

WHEN FAHAD AND ALI were driving in the car, the seats inches apart, or when they were on a charpayee on the terrace by the landing in the evening, on the grubby seats at the cinema, leaning out of the sunroof by the airbase watching jets land and take off, the space between their bodies was like a vertiginous drop drawing Fahad nearer. And it was the fear of what must happen, what must must must, that made his breath catch in his throat.

Sometimes they were so near that Fahad could feel the heat from Ali's skin. But even though they sat side by side on his bed, their backs against the wall, their knees tipping towards each other, the fattest parts of their arms pressed together, there remained a distance between them that could never be crossed, a gulf somehow within Fahad too, hollowing him with a hunger that could never be satisfied.

So he began avoiding Ali. 'Tell him I'm not feeling well,' Fahad instructed the servants. 'Tell him I'm with my father.' And when he heard Ali coming up the stairs, Fahad hid on the terrace till he left.

He reminded himself of all he didn't like about Ali, the funny things he said when he spoke in English—'pizza' like it was the city with the tower, America for anywhere further west than Istanbul, 'how is it' when he meant 'how are you'— that he was dark as a peasant, that he had lips like a girl.

Fahad didn't sleep at night. He saw Ali's face on the ceiling. The walls of the house burned like a tandoor. Fahad turned and turned in his bed till the damp sheets wound round him like binding. The time passed unbearably slowly. There was a feeling in the house of death. There was, there was. The dust hung in the air—it didn't move. Once he heard a dog howl outside as though it were dying. It was the most terrible sound he'd ever heard, the most plaintive, the most desperate cry for help—and he fought every urge in his body to run downstairs, to unbolt the door, to find it wherever it was. Instead, he told himself, It will stop, it will stop. But it continued for an hour perhaps, maybe longer, maybe only minutes, the cry becoming fainter but more desperate, fainter still, fainter till it was the tiniest sound imaginable and then it was gone. He remembered the dog they had run over on the road, the body bundled up in the beam of their lights. It was cruel, he told himself. He's cruel. He is. But what had happened out there that night didn't seem cruel for some reason. It seemed like a sacrifice.

I will be better, he told himself. I will, I will, I will. But what did that even mean?

One day, after weeks of this, he tried to see how long he could go without speaking—and lasted nine hours, till late afternoon, when the words and thoughts in his head and mouth spun him into delirium and he thought he might never speak again if he didn't speak then. He ran to the terrace, round

the corner of a wall, where the parapet overlooked a cluster of servants' quarters, and shouted into the crook of his
arm—hello, hello, help, halo, hallow, how low—sobbing and
shaking.

Once, he stood at the top of the staircase and willed his
knees to buckle.

Once, he held his glass under the running tap, water filling
it to the brim, and considered drinking. His father, the manager, the servants had warned him against it, that it was sour
with poison from the open sewers, the runoff of pesticides,
that the sickness it caused lasted months. He'd raised the
glass to his lips, felt the water like warm fingers against them,
but hadn't been able to bring himself to open his mouth.

He couldn't read the book he'd taken from his mother—
each delicious sentence stung. He couldn't read at all, because he'd think of Ali sitting in the armchair, watching him
read, though by then, Ali had stopped coming to the house.

'It's good,' the servants said. 'These aren't good people.
Now his father wants the seat for himself. Now he's telling
people, "The two cousins will run each other into the ground.
If this family cannot sort its troubles, what can it do?"'

There had been skirmishes on the lands. Men had died.
Men of his father's and men of Mousey's. 'What can we do?'
his father had said. 'Give them a little money and they'll be
quiet. They do this to themselves.'

But Fahad couldn't not think about Ali. He couldn't,
he couldn't, he couldn't. He was weak and he couldn't and he
punched his legs and his chest with his fist like a child. You're
a child, he told himself—but he wasn't and he wished he was.

He would leave. He would leave and never come back.
That was what he would do.

EIGHT

BUT FAHAD DIDN'T LEAVE. Instead he went one evening to the Greenland Hotel for ice cream. Perhaps he was hoping. Perhaps he was. The ice cream's sweetness was a thrill now, it thrummed through his teeth as if he were gnawing a bone. He went again, and then again, and as he was waiting for his order in the car, the battered Suzuki swam into view in the reflective glare of the window.

'You've only ordered one?' Ali said. 'You only think of yourself? Because you have a small family.'

Fahad shouted out to the waiter to bring another. He climbed into Ali's car. He tapped the Koran hanging from the rearview mirror so that it swung.

'You weren't well?' Ali said.

Fahad shrugged. He felt his cheeks become hot and bent his face over his lap. Ali put his hand on Fahad's back.

'To be a friend,' Ali said, 'is to be a brother.'

The ice cream stuck in Fahad's throat and he began to cough and Ali slammed his hand against Fahad's back again, again, again.

'You're enjoying it,' Fahad said, once he could talk. 'You're a thug.'

'What else?' Ali said.

They shared a plate of masala chips and another of cheese pakoras. Fahad sent his driver home—he'd come back with Ali, he said.

'OUR FARMERS ARE SHOOTING each other,' Fahad said.

'You don't see it,' Ali said. 'Your father is fighting for everything. It's like a war. You can't see it.'

'People say your father wants the seat now.'

'People say anything they want,' Ali said. Then he added, 'I am not my father.'

He told a story about his sister, that she'd run away with a man from a village in the neighbouring district. They'd gone with guns and brought her back. But she'd run away again. 'Rafik Sahib helped us,' he said. 'He knew the chief of the tribe.' Ali gave his name, he'd been a minister at the same time as Fahad's grandfather. 'She came with the man to the house of this chief. In such dirty clothes. The man was a drunkard, he was a gambler. Ask anyone.' He knocked the plate with his knee and pakoras scattered across Fahad's lap. 'In our house, we looked after her. Not like that. Rafik Sahib told her to come back. She said, "No." He asked three, four times. He said, "What do you want to do? Do you want to stay where you are?" "Yes," she said.'

He tossed a couple of hundred rupee notes at the waiter hovering outside, started the car, and reversed, a man on a bike swooping out of the way. 'It's good,' he continued. 'Her value was this before'—he spread his arms wide—'but after the nikkah, not even this.' He pinched his fingers together. 'What could we have done? But the man, if I see him, I'll kill him.' She was his favourite sister, he said. She was the most beautiful, the loveliest. 'A face like an angel,' he said. Then, 'What are angels' faces? A face so darling'—he stroked his fingers along the line of his jaw—'and someone so kind, so generous, so wise. More of a mother to me than my mother. More of a father to me than my father.' He'd wanted her to choose a wife for him. He didn't trust himself. He'd have trusted her with anything. He looked at Fahad. He seemed unable to look away, till a truck driving the wrong way blared its horn and he swerved to avoid it.

'I'll decide whatever I want,' Fahad said. 'I will.' So that he didn't look at Ali, he looked out of the window, at the Christian graveyard with its rusted gate hanging off its hinges, at a pair of worn sandals abandoned outside, at a white seam of salt threading across the crumbling bricks in the wall, at the tall yellowing grass growing in a ditch—and their faces reflected so imperfectly in the glass that he couldn't see which was which.

How did they even meet though, Fahad asked, Ali's sister and the man she ran away with?

Ali didn't know.

How did love happen here, Fahad continued, if only the village girls came out of their houses uncovered?

Fahad could have any of the girls from the villages on the family's lands that he wanted, Ali said, winking at Fahad in the rearview mirror, making his lips into the shape of a kiss.

He didn't want them, Fahad said. He turned away, wound the window down, closed his eyes and the hot air whipped at his face.

'The village girls from Abad are famous,' Ali said. 'People come from all over.'

'No they don't,' Fahad said.

'You're very difficult,' Ali said. 'You have all these nakhras. I don't know why.' He slowed the car and spun it round in the middle of the road. 'Come,' he said. 'We'll find one for you.'

'No,' Fahad said. 'I don't want to.'

'It's just having fun,' Ali said. He pushed a cassette into the deck, suddenly merry, and sang along to a song he liked. 'Don't ask me,' he sang, 'to love you as I loved you before.' He had a beautiful voice and Fahad told him to stop. He chucked Fahad on the chin. 'What is there in the world, but your eyes?'

'Maybe she loved him,' Fahad said, 'your sister. Why shouldn't she stay with him?'

He continued singing. When the song finished, he said, 'How could she know him? We knew what he was—a drunkard, a gambler. He tricked her—what else? Many people were jealous because she was so beautiful. It attracts envy, ill wishes. It's better to be plain.'

'People fall in love,' Fahad said.

'What do you know, little baba?' Ali said.

There was a way from the road that led through a wasteland to the tail end of the canal where Mousey's land began and Ali took this route, the tyres spinning clouds of yellow dust up around the car. There was no track here, there were bushes and boulders to navigate around and, in the distance, trees and the village where Fahad had distributed sweets earlier in the summer.

They bounced across the uneven earth, Ali racing wherever there was an uninterrupted stretch. That day for some reason there were no wild dogs as they approached the village. Its gates were shut, bound together with coarse rope.

They drove around the perimeter. The cakes of dung that ordinarily pocked the surface of the walls had been smoothed away. The walls were low enough that they could easily see into a cluster of earthen dwellings around a yard. What was the point of such low walls, Fahad wanted to know.

Ali shrugged. 'Each year, these walls will move a little further out. Only so much.' He pressed his fingers together. 'Of course they must. These farmers have children, and their children have children.'

The dwellings were small and dark, open at the front like mouths. In the yard between them, there were tall clay mounds. Silos for grain, Ali said, pointing out where they had been broken open and emptied.

The place was desolate.

'It's a war,' Ali said. 'Perhaps an elder was killed. If they stay, they must take a life for the one they lost and lose one again and take one. It goes on for years sometimes.'

He steered the car up onto the steep bank at the end of the canal. 'All for this,' he said. The canal was dry—the concrete lining of the walls pitted, the bed caked with blood-coloured earth and scattered with rubbish, pink and green plastic bags fine as onion skin, and strands of tinsel. A single goat—abandoned? lost?—skittered along and up and down the walls, pecking in the dirt for food. The fields on either side were rocky, streaked with limp browning grass.

'It's finished,' Ali said. 'This paddy. Nobody will get money for it.' Plastic bags swirled across the fields too, catching here and there amongst the stony clods. 'What will these people do for money, for food? They must already have sold the animals they have. This is their savings account. When the harvest is good, they buy a buffalo, then another, and slowly there are more.'

'If they have savings, it isn't so bad. They won't go hungry,' Fahad said.

'Bad or not, they have no choice,' Ali said. 'What is a man without choice?'

It was strange to see no one about, no brightly coloured figures in the fields or clustered in the shade of a tree for rest.

NINE

THEY TURNED OFF the canal road. They drove around. 'It's like an apocalypse,' Fahad said. 'It's like a war zone. It's like Carthage.' There were no animals about—the birds were gone. The heat was fiercest of all here and Fahad's clothes were damp with sweat, his body slicked with it. Fahad remembered the temple, told Ali what he'd seen there.

'Again this story,' Ali said. 'You've told me ten times.'

'The manager saw it all too,' Fahad said.

You wouldn't find big cats here anymore, Ali said. 'You thought it was big because you were frightened.'

'It was,' Fahad said. He showed Ali with his hands. 'Big as this. Bigger. With teeth long as fingers.' He curved his forefingers from his lips.

'How did you see? You said there was blood across the mouth. You didn't say the mouth was open.'

'It was,' Fahad said, doubting himself now. Was it? But he could see it clearly as though he were there again. 'It isn't a temple at all. I don't know why they call it that. It's only trees and a grave.'

'The grave of a saint is a temple,' Ali said.

In the distance, in the direction they were going, smoke plumed into the sky.

'Something is happening,' Fahad said. 'It doesn't look right. Turn around. Here—here—' He indicated a path to the left barely wide enough for a donkey cart.

But Ali kept going. The track led up a steep incline and as they approached the top of it, the canal came into view. A crowd had gathered at a particular spot on the bank and a thick column of smoke rose into the air. The men were waving crooks and shouting.

'The other way,' Fahad said. 'Into the field.'

But there was nowhere to go.

'The tyres will stick—' Ali's voice was unnaturally slow. He crept forward in the same direction. 'It must be your farmers,' he said. 'His farmers.' He stopped. They were several car lengths away but now the crowd surged towards them.

They roared and shook their sticks, their faces distorted, their mouths enormous. Ali reached across Fahad and locked his door. Each stick was thick as a man's leg and the farmers struck the ground with them so that it shook, so that the car trembled, the plastic Koran hanging from the rearview mirror swung, sunlight sparking off its corners.

He wasn't afraid, Fahad told himself. He wasn't afraid but he wasn't not afraid—the crowd rushing nearer—and those weren't all sticks, there were guns too. He was and he wasn't.

'From where have they got these pistols and rifles?' Ali said.

He was and he wasn't—like his fear was inside something that was inside him, like something buoyant, like he'd rise into the air if the roof weren't holding him down. He raised his hands, flattened them against the roof, as if to stop himself.

They were all around now, darkening the windows, thudding their fists against the chassis, drumming the bonnet, shouting things he didn't understand. Fahad imagined himself sliding the sunroof open, standing up, looking out over them, addressing them, his voice ringing above the din.

'What are you doing?' Ali grabbed at Fahad's arm. 'Don't open it.'

They struggled, then suddenly the car jerked forward, again, again, some of the people ahead falling out of the way. A tractor tyre was burning ahead, flames writhing like dancing men. They skidded towards it and then swerved aside, the back of the car slipping at the edge of the bank, racing in the dirt, the crowd roaring after them, the car bouncing over a ditch, over a log, over a mound of earth.

'What were you thinking?' Ali said. 'You were opening the roof.'

'I don't know,' Fahad said. 'I was just doing it. I was going to say something.'

'But you don't speak the language.'

'I know.'

'There was a Kalashnikov,' Ali said. 'They could have fired.' He stopped the car. They turned to look back, their shoulders twisting together, their cheeks side by side.

The men were too far to make out faces. Now the crowd was a mass that could have been a truck or a wall or a boulder or a cloud so low it touched the ground.

'You were opening the roof,' Ali said again. 'You've lost your mind.'

Fahad climbed out of the car. 'I have to move,' he said, jogging his feet on the spot. 'I feel all this—' And he kicked dirt up with his heels.

'You've gone mad,' Ali said, getting out too, watching him, one hand over the rim of the open window.

Fahad picked up stones and tossed them into the brimming canal. 'I'll drive,' he said, and pushed past Ali into the driver's seat. 'I have to do something. I can't just sit.'

He raced down the track. Here it was like another place entirely—the fields were golden, the paddy bowing with the weight of heavy ears of grain. 'In a night it's gone from green to gold,' he said—there were rippling oceans of it. 'I've never been so happy,' Fahad shouted. 'Never, never, never.'

They neared a village and children came pouring out of the open gates. 'We have no toffees,' he shouted through the window, waving his hand. 'We have nothing,' and sped past them.

'I'll take you somewhere,' he told Ali, who was laughing, who was jogging his knees, and they crossed the canal, took this turn, then that, then round the side of the little graveyard. How well he knew his way around now.

'How well I know my way,' he said, 'where everywhere is.'

'And you should,' Ali said. 'It's your land.'

'It's not mine,' Fahad said. 'It's my father's.'

'The same,' Ali said. 'To those farmers'—he nodded back the way they'd come—'you think you are any different from your father?'

Fahad parked the car at the top of the path that led to the temple. 'I'll show you,' he told Ali. 'It's here—' But he didn't say what it was or what he'd show him. Still, when he looked back, Ali was tripping after him, the paddy stalks tugging at his clothes, tugging his collar open.

'Come,' he shouted at Ali, who had fallen behind. At the edge of the copse, Fahad waited for him to catch up. Every tree was different from the other: one kind of palm here with a thorny trunk, another there with a smooth trunk, a giant tree with dark fleshy leaves the size of a hand, something like a banyan with branches hanging vertically like hair, its vines coiling about the various trunks knitting them all together. The earth was soft as mulch, almost black, a clod of soil breaking into beetles as he trod on it.

'Now where is this lion,' Ali said, putting a hand on Fahad's shoulder, allowing it to slip down his back, onto the small of his back.

'It's a different smell here even,' Fahad said—whispering, he didn't know why. The air was damp with a cloying, intimate sweetness, like overripe papayas. 'She was there—' He pointed at the bush where he'd seen the cat but didn't go nearer.

'Is she there now?' Ali said.

'And the tomb is here—' Fahad continued along the path to where it ended at a little clearing in front of the plastered green walls of the mausoleum. In the window openings, shards of mirrored glass hung on threads, tinkling together in the still air, though no breeze blew.

'Sometimes, it's like you're my brother,' Ali said. 'Sometimes, like my sister.' He laughed and pinched the tender part of Fahad's side.

'Like your prettiest sister?' Fahad said. 'Like your favourite sister?' He began to dance as he'd danced in the school play, turning his wrists out, pivoting his hip to one side, kicking his sandals off his feet, and raising his heel. 'Sing something,' he said—and Ali sang that song again.

'Do not ask me, my love, for the love I had before.'

Fahad spun on his heel.

'You are here, so life is radiant.'

Fahad bowed his head. He stamped circles in the soft earth in the shape of his feet. He clapped his hands and tilted his head to this side then that.

'What is life's sorrow when to ache for you is enough?' Ali's voice was louder here amongst the leaves and branches. It was as though there was music accompanying him.

Fahad turned and turned and reached his arms out like wings, as though if he spun fast enough, he would spin into the air. But the spinning unsteadied him and he toppled onto Ali, Ali catching him in an embrace, squeezing him one way then another, as though they were tussling.

And suddenly it seemed that everything was allowed—for Fahad to tug loose the knot that tied Ali's salwar, for him to press his palm against the soft hairs on Ali's flank, for him to dip his head into the nook between Ali's neck and shoulder—and, in turn, that he must allow everything too—for Ali to twist Fahad's arm behind him, to bend him backwards, to knock one of Fahad's heels away from the ground and lower him onto his back.

Kissing was teeth knocking, faces that didn't fit, it was the same with their bodies, grappling with each other, tumbling onto the forest floor, a stone digging into Fahad's temple, crumbs of soil finding their way into his mouth, and at some point he became afraid and it was like they were fighting, like he was having to surrender, like these were acts of violence they were perpetrating one upon the other, that to hook his fingers round Ali's shoulder blade, to twist his ankle round Ali's calf, that for Ali to cradle Fahad's head in his palm, to shift his hips between Fahad's legs, that these were threats of force, that they could not make gifts of their bodies one to the other because their bodies were not theirs to give.

Light sparked between the leaves and now Fahad was floating above his body because it wasn't really happening, it wasn't, it wasn't, and he didn't dare to speak in case it broke the spell, he didn't dare to be himself in any recognisable way, wanted desperately to hide but desperately never to leave. There was a moment when he was afraid and he curled up into himself like a shell—and there was a moment when he watched himself dispassionately from above, his body twisting into the dirt.

And then after, they lay together, their arms slung casually across one another, loosely crossed, and there was music again in that little forest, birdsong tinkling like wind chimes and the delicate percussion of the leaves moving with the branches.

'It's like Iftar,' Ali said, 'eating after being hungry so long.' Was there anything so pure as love? he said. Was there anything so noble? It was like—like—like—and he couldn't think of things it was like.

Their breaths rose and fell in their bodies at the same time.

'Yes,' Fahad said, to hear his own voice, to hear it thrum across Ali's chest, 'yes. This saint is not so bad as everyone says.' He glanced across at the low green building, at a triangle of light between the windows on the opposite wall. Around his neck on a fine gold chain Ali wore an engraved pendant and Fahad felt the letters across it with the tip of his

finger, wound the chain around his finger. 'If time could stop,'
he said, 'and never go on, I would be happy forever.'

'You're a poet,' Ali said. 'If time stopped, you'd still get
tired, you'd still get hungry or thirsty or fed up or angry.'

'No,' Fahad said. 'If time stopped everything would stay
exactly as it is.'

BUT AS THEY LAY THERE, they drifted apart somehow, as
though they had been one thing and now became two. Ali's
arms were damp with sweat. Fahad moved his own away.
The bristle of hair on Ali's legs scratched. The smell of him
reached down Fahad's throat and made him retch.

It was Ali, it wasn't anybody else, Fahad told himself, but
as he turned to look at Ali, Ali was somebody else, someone
grotesque, deformed as a gargoyle, as though by a trick of
the light scattering through the copse Fahad could finally see
him for who he was.

A branch snapped somewhere on the ground behind
them—a purposeful sound that made them sit up and turn
their heads in the direction they'd come. And then a series of
sounds across the forest floor—of crushing leaves and twigs
breaking. 'Something is moving,' Ali said. 'The cat, it must be
your lion,' he added with a forced lightness.

They scrambled for their clothes, Fahad putting his arm
into the wrong sleeve, hearing his shirt rip as he wrenched
it round, Ali struggling to tie his salwar. And then the two
of them hurrying out of the copse, Fahad searching wildly
for whatever it was that had made that sound, that sounded
larger, more wilful, than a lion.

There was some relief emerging from the forest into the

field, swiping the tall copper grass aside. Was someone moving ahead? Was that the sound of an engine firing? Stones bit
into the soles of his feet and Fahad realised he had forgotten
his sandals. He called out to Ali but they kept moving forward.
They scrambled up the verge to where they'd parked. In the
distance there was a spot that could be a cloud of dust, that
could be a car speeding away.

'Is it a car?' Fahad said.

'Is it a jeep?' Ali said. 'The green one? But it's too far. It
didn't come from here. It must have come another way.' His
voice rose at the end as though he were asking a question.

A drop of water spattered against Fahad's neck, another
on his cheek. It began to rain. They climbed into the car and
at once the rain fell too heavily for them to see. They edged
forward, seeing the road in flashes as the wipers spun side to
side. The track rose up towards the canal bank and the tyres
began to slide, to race in the mud. The sheets of rain were
thick and close as walls—and how near was the canal, Fahad
couldn't see. 'Not so close,' Fahad shouted, grabbing at the
wheel to steer the car to the right. The rain drumming on the
roof, on the windscreen, Fahad's skin sticky with it, his shirt
streaked with mud. 'My shirt,' he said.

He wanted to be out of those clothes and out of that car
and out of his body but it seemed as though the car were
barely moving. 'Go,' Fahad said. 'What are you doing?'

'I'm being careful,' Ali said softly. 'I can't see. If you can
see, you drive.' He stopped, and they swapped places, their
clothes and hair plastered to their skin now, the car steaming.

Why should Fahad care whether they drove into the canal
or tumbled off the bank into the field? It would be better, it
would.

'You can't see,' Ali said. 'You're too fast.' He laid his hand on Fahad's arm and Fahad—for some reason, for some reason he didn't know—shrugged it off.

And still he raced and then they were bouncing down the track that led home, and then swinging round the walls, the tyres spraying up mud in thick clods. The house was a different place in the rain—the yard obscured entirely, a wall dissolving into water, the porch appearing suddenly and not where he'd expected it. He hurried out without saying anything to Ali. He had to see his father first—why?

The rain and damp clouded through the hallways as well, leaving a fog of condensation across windowpanes and mirrors. He called out to his father and heard his voice echo. He shouted down the corridor, into the drawing room, into his father's bedroom. He shouted up the stairs, across the landing, even out on the terrace, from where he saw Ali's car still waiting, beginning now, slowly, to reverse.

The servants were lounging on their charpayees under the awning outside the kitchen, smoking, watching the water sluice off the eaves. His father was with Mousey, they said. Mousey had called him to his house. It was good, they said. They were happy. These troubles would be in the past. The cousins would reconcile.

TEN

IT HAD BEGUN to rain while Rafik was in the jeep—drops fat as locusts. It made him laugh and laugh and double up laughing.

'But it's the wrong time for rain,' the old driver said, glancing at him. 'It isn't good at all.'

It was—it was a terrible time for rain, too late for his crop and too, too late for Mousey's—Mousey's was long gone—and that was why he laughed and held his hands up to show how helpless they all were, how completely at God's mercy. 'Who do we think we are?' he said. 'We're nothing at all.'

'The banks will overflow,' the driver said. 'The crop will be flooded. Ours too.'

That made Rafik laugh even more. 'We will have to leave in boats,' he said, slapping his leg. 'We will turn the doors into rafts.'

AFTER HIS FATHER had died, Mumtaz Chacha had left the house to Rafik and built his own much more lavish, much more private house on the other side of the lands. It was in a style that was new even now for Abad—several stories of sand-coloured concrete piled seemingly haphazardly on top of each other. Mousey had added a high hedge wall that concealed the house entirely from the outside.

The gatekeeper had apparently abandoned his post to the rain. After sounding the horn several times, Rafik's driver climbed out of the car, hurried to the gate, holding his hands over his head, only to find that it was bolted from the inside. He returned to the car, sounded the horn again. 'Perhaps he is not here,' he said, water streaming down his cheeks. He dabbed at his face with a tissue and it left scraps on his nose and forehead, flecks in his beard. Rafik leaned across him, leaned heavily on the horn, held his fist there.

Then the gate shook and one half swung open, then the other and they were waved in. On either side of the driveway was a garden of tall flowering bushes. His uncle's lawn had disappeared. Trees in giant pots were stacked along the verandah where people would have sat—olive trees that weren't suited to this climate at all.

'These won't last,' he told the servant who opened the door for him, shaking the rainwater out of his hair, tugging his shirt loose by its collar. 'You tell your master.' The house was different from the inside too—he couldn't tell how at first. But it was the walls, there were photographs from floor to ceiling: Mumtaz Chacha with the shah, with the old Aga Khan, with various tribal leaders, and here was Mousey in some local government office, here he was as a boy with his father and Ayub Khan and here as a boy in his father's arms, his father handing him to someone out of view, the boy's arms and legs dangling as though he were a puppet, as though there were no life in him at all.

Mousey appeared silently at the bottom of the stairs, his arms crossed behind his back, the way his father would.

Rafik waved his hand at the walls, meaning to say that it was all new, that it was all different, that it was all Mousey's doing. Neither of them spoke.

Mousey looked around as if searching for someone. Then he turned and Rafik followed him to the drawing room.

They sat. In his head, Rafik had already said a hundred things. 'You are the son of my father's brother,' he had said. He had said this many times. In his head, he had taken Mousey's hand from behind his back and clasped it. 'I forgive you,' he had said.

The rain fell harder. It drummed against the walls and the windows.

The bearer appeared with tea. He stirred three spoonfuls of sugar into it. He set the cup and saucer in front of Rafik. Rafik tipped the tea into the saucer and sipped it. He signalled at the window, as if to say, 'God has decided for us. Who are we? Nothing at all. Nothing at all.'

'It's a godawful place,' Mousey said finally. 'It's a hellhole. God knows why people fight for this. For this? Take it all. It will bury you. But you can't see a thing.'

His voice wasn't at all as Rafik had remembered. It had a coarseness to it—like his father's had. A wilfulness.

'It's our land,' Rafik said. 'What can we do?'

'I sold the London apartment,' Mousey said, shaking his head.

'Cadogan Gardens,' Rafik said. 'Your father died here

in the room at the back—' He gestured at the wall. 'In the last week, he didn't open his eyes even but one time—' He held up a finger. 'He was looking and looking.' He nodded at Mousey. 'He was looking for you. What else?' He poured more tea into his saucer, sipped noisily. '"He's coming," I said. "He's coming."'

'Of course,' Mousey said, 'you were like the son. That must make you happy as well. You must be a very happy man. Aren't you? Happy all the time. Having everything you want. And what will you do with it all? Buried under it like Midas.'

'It was jungle,' Rafik said. 'All this, there was nothing here.'

'Very good,' Mousey said. 'Well done.'

Water gushed from the roof, thick streams curtaining the windows.

'Once we were like brothers,' Rafik said.

'There are brothers and there are brothers,' Mousey said. 'I know which kind you are.'

'There is only one kind,' Rafik said. 'It means but one thing.'

A young man appeared in the doorway, glanced in, frowned at Rafik before salaaming him. Mousey waved him away.

'From the start, you wanted me gone,' Mousey said. 'You cooked up that whole drama when we were boys. You goaded me and goaded me, spreading lies so that people called me names.'

'You're forgetting,' Rafik said. 'What you do is your business. I was the one telling people to show some respect.'

'Respect,' Mousey said. 'Yes, yes. Your respect,' he continued, 'it will sting a man like poison. I begged you, I didn't want to be sent away. "Speak to them," I said. "Speak to your father, speak to mine. They listen to you." God knows why they listened to you. You pulled the wool over everyone's eyes. Going like a snake from one to the next.' He moved his arm to mime that serpent motion. 'And these people here, that look up to you like a saint. They have nothing. All they can get, they can get from only you. And see how you've treated them. Starving them of water so that they lose their crop.'

'These people tell you they have nothing,' Rafik said. 'They have herds and herds of buffalo. One buffalo you can sell for thirty thousand. Just imagine.'

'All the business that happened, nothing happened at all, but it was you, you wanted me gone.' Mousey's voice had begun to shake. He stood and it seemed as though he were trembling. 'What did I do to deserve to be sent away? It was all your doing, your whispering here and there to your father, to my father, about this and that, that there would be trouble, that I should go. From the start you were like that, always afraid of me.'

'Mousey,' Rafik said, and gestured at him to sit.

'What name should I call you?' Mousey said. 'Everywhere you tried to undermine me. At school even, it was you telling people I was this, I was that. And now still saying God knows what. Why do you care? Concern yourself with yourself. Why am I your business? Always, always, always worrying about me. Even then, even as a boy, you were thinking how could you have everything. It wasn't enough for you to have what your father had. You must have everything. Cosying up to my father. *My* father. You wouldn't even allow me the love of my own father. What was he to you?'

There was a noise outside—the sound of the front door,

footsteps, voices. Then someone burst into the room—Fahad, his hair plastered to his head, his clothes wound round him, water streaming from the hem of his kurta. His shirt was streaked with mud.

He was barefoot. He stopped just beyond the threshold. Mousey frowned at him, then at Rafik. He called out for a towel, and the young man Rafik had seen before reappeared with one and patted it around Fahad's shoulders.

Fahad wrenched it from him.

'What were you saying?' he said to Mousey. 'What were you talking about?' He turned wildly to his father. 'You came in the jeep,' he said. 'Why did you take the jeep? Why not the big car?'

'Sit down, baba,' Rafik said.

Fahad pressed the towel to his face, then tossed it onto the carpet. He walked towards an armchair and stood behind it.

'What were you saying?' he said. 'Why did you stop talking when I came in?' He wiped his hair out of his eyes. 'You were saying something about me,' he said to Mousey. Then to Rafik, 'Did he say something about me? Don't believe anything he says. And him—' He pointed at the young man who hovered still in the doorway. 'Why is he here?'

'Your clothes are soaked through,' Mousey said. 'Take him upstairs'—he addressed this to the young man—'and find him something else to wear.'

'He won't take me anywhere,' Fahad said.

'You go back to the house,' Rafik said, 'with my driver. I'll drive myself.'

'You know he sleeps in the house?' Fahad said. 'Isn't that strange? That the manager should sleep in the house? Does he have a different bedroom? How many bedrooms are there? Show me. I want to see them.'

It was a strange silence that descended upon them—a dense shroud that muffled everything, every thought, every word that could be spoken, every gesture that could be made—silence but for the insistent drumming of the rain, which seemed to say again and again, what must be, what must be, what must be, must be, must be.

Finally, the boy crumpled into the chair, lifeless as a doll.

Mousey called for kava for him. He called to the bearer to bring clothes, that he could wear them here if he wouldn't go anywhere else. The young man remained at the door.

'Who is this?' Rafik said. Then he asked the man who he was.

He was Mousey's manager, he said. Rafik had done wonders with the lands, he said. He remembered as a child that there were only forests here, that there were hills and ditches. He remembered people saying it would never be farmland, the cost was too high, it would bankrupt the family before it made them any money.

'People thought I was mad. They told your father,' Rafik said to Mousey, '"What have you done, giving this boy the charge of the lands?" Your father said, "He has borrowed money himself. It's his responsibility." Your father said to me, "I won't pay your debts. If you can't afford to, you sell whatever you have. I'll buy it," he said. He was a sharp one. He was a funny one.'

'But, sir,' the young man continued, 'allow a father to give to a son. A father who gave nothing in his life, allow him to give something after. Allow him that.'

'This seed,' Rafik said, 'you cannot reuse it. You use it once and then you have to buy new seed. Do you understand?'

Mousey was looking at Fahad, and Fahad was looking at his hands, upturned on his lap. How similar they were, Rafik thought, and found the thought so distasteful, so bitter in his mouth, he gulped what tea remained straight from the cup. 'Good, good,' he said to Mousey. 'All good and well.' Whatever it was to be, let it be that, let it be that.

They were all standing now.

'Your father didn't care for you,' Rafik said. 'I'm sorry to tell you that. There was no love lost, as they say.'

Mousey grabbed Rafik by the collar. They tussled, Mousey summoning some tremendous strength from God knows where, dragging Rafik out of the drawing room, out of the hallway, Rafik losing one of his shoes, Mousey throwing him—yes, throwing him—out of the door. Rafik would have fallen but for a post that he caught on to, swung to one side of.

Fahad appeared with Rafik's missing shoe, kneeled and lifted Rafik's foot into it. He took Rafik by the arm and walked him to the big car, ordering the driver to take the little jeep back, shouting to be heard across the heavy rain.

'All of us sons,' Rafik said. 'But no fathers.'

The mirrors and windows fogged up and Fahad wiped the windscreen clean with the cuff of his shirt. The smell of damp was like earth pressed against the face.

The rain had washed the roads to sludge. The tyres slipped and raced and spattered mud up against the windows. The car slid along the road.

'Why did you come like this?' Rafik said.

The car slid towards the verge and started to spin.

'I didn't know where you were,' the boy said.

'You knew. You came here.'

'I followed you,' the boy said slowly. 'I didn't know what else to do.'

'I stood in the grave when his father was being buried,' Rafik said. 'They put his body in my arms and I laid him to rest. People didn't know who the son was. They didn't know there was one.'

'Why is it the thing that everyone wants?' the boy said. 'Why does it matter? But it does. It's the only thing that does.'

'I should have knocked his daylights out,' Rafik said. 'I should have him thrown in jail. You watch yourself or you'll end up like him.'

'But how do you know what you want?' the boy said. 'How do you choose? I don't know how. And if it fills my head? If there's nothing else but that? How do I choose something else?'

'No, no, you'll be alright—' Rafik squeezed him by the shoulder 'You're the cleverest of all. You use this.' He tapped his temple.

The boy had a strange look to his face, eyes wide as though he'd seen something terrible. 'Ali—' the boy said. The car slid slowly backwards.

'Ali?'

'Whose father owns the pump.'

'They're all thugs,' Rafik said.

The back of the car swung off the path, onto the embankment. The boy ground the gears. 'Use the four-wheel.' Rafik showed him. The car tipped backwards.

'It's good that you have a friend,' Rafik said.

'It's strange here,' Fahad said. The front tyres had lifted off the ground. 'It's very strange. I don't know what I think.'

II

ELEVEN

MOUSEY WAS DEAD and that was that. The man who had called to tell Rafik cried as though there were something that could be done, calling Mousey his brother. Brother hadn't made a sound, the man said, so he likely hadn't felt a thing, wasn't that right, that he hadn't suffered?

Brother slept like a statue, with the covers wrapped tightly round him. They hadn't thought a thing was wrong. His lips were spread as though he were smiling. But he hadn't answered when they'd called out to him, not even when they were close, and then they'd seen a thread of yellow vomit hanging from the corner of his mouth and they'd touched their hand to his shoulder, they'd shaken him gently, then more roughly, then they'd shouted out.

Rafik thought for some reason of the boy, who'd been gone, how long, ten, twenty years now.

It was summer and with the power cutting every hour for an hour there was nowhere to keep Brother, the body would start to smell soon.

'Then wash him,' Rafik said. They'd bury him that eve-ning as soon as Rafik could get to Abad.

It wasn't a good time. Conversations were being had in the capital about the current administration, was it working or no? Did the PM need more time to prove himself, or no? Was a tougher sort needed to steer the ship through these rocky waters, the Indians causing trouble in Afghanistan, the Rus-sians bruised and belligerent, and the Americans, the Ameri-cans worst of all, never to be trusted. And was Rafik just that tougher sort, this one and that coming to see him, generals and chief justices, dissenting members of the cabinet, the opposition, the US ambassador, so that he didn't have time to think of Mousey, not even on the journey to Abad, not even as he stepped inside Mousey's house or climbed the stairs to Mousey's bedroom.

Finally, when Rafik saw him on the bed, he did not recog-nise his cousin. He was bound in white muslin, white muslin wrapped around his head, close as a wimple. He was grey as mud, with deep lines under his cheeks and along his jaw. The corners of his eyes drooped, as though his face were sliding off his skull.

'Is it him?' Rafik said to the man who'd brought him there.

The man didn't understand and Rafik waved him away. He wanted to say something to Mousey in that moment but could think of nothing that meant anything. Again, he thought of the boy, imagined the boy by his side, the two of them in complicit silence.

Rafik buried Mousey beside Mumtaz Chacha on a bluff overlooking the lands. Thousands had gathered—more than had come for Chacha, or even Rafik's father. A sea of figures surged behind Rafik—the sound they made like the roar of waves.

The paddy was high as a man, thousands of verdant acres, and beyond, in the very distant distance, were the smoking chimneys of Rafik's various mills and gins. Standing there, his father in the ground to one side, his uncle and cousin to the other, and the ocean swell of an army behind him, he imagined he could step off the edge of that rocky cliff and the breeze like a palanquin would carry him out over an endless empire.

Roads had been built by the money he'd sent back to Abad, blacktops gleaming like rivers of oil. And there was a water purification plant that had cost a billion, there was a hospital, there were schools. The local government officers wanted to show it all to him, but he had no time.

MOUSEY HAD LEFT him a letter, almost as though he had known this was coming.

Brother had written it only a few days ago, that manservant of Mousey's told him, and propped it up on his desk with Rafik's name on the envelope. 'Wasn't that a strange thing to do?' Again, the man's voice warbling, again his hands before his face as if in prayer.

Of course, all these servants were worried about their jobs. He'd keep the house running as it was, Rafik said, for guests or visitors, for the time being, though it made no sense. No guests or visitors would come.

It was a curious letter, Mousey's thoughts barely coherent. 'We hold on to things as if we own them, putting people in boxes, and places too. Nothing is big enough but this house, this house there's only space I wanted to fill. I think a lot about the past. What should I do with those thoughts? You who are the master of everything tell me that.' In a later section he had written, the shapes of his letters becoming less precise, wavering from the line, 'I forgive you, I forgive you, I forgive you. It is a powerful thing to do and I do it. I do it a hundred times because for you once isn't enough.'

It concluded finally with two requests. 'How many thousands come to you for favours every week,' he had written, 'and all I ask for is two. Everything is yours now. Land, land, more land. Coming out of your ears. What can a man do with so much land? I promised a hundred acres to—' Here he had written a name Rafik did not recognise. 'Give it to him. Any contiguous piece from what belonged to me as you see fit, though I had in mind the long band that curves away from that odd little copse up to the tail end of the canal. It is no better or worse than any other stretch of land, only that it has some sentimental value to me.' The second request related to the boy. Mousey had been fond of him. 'Tell Fahad this story from your mouth. After all these years away, he must come back to Abad now. London will always be there. Tell him it was my dream that he would return. Why? God only knows.' It was jarring—as though Mousey were speaking to the thoughts in Rafik's head.

Rafik asked for the man whose name Mousey had given in his letter and discovered it was the servant standing in front of him, the man who'd found the letter on Mousey's desk and brought it here now. The man wiped his eyes against his cuff—he was wearing a shirt and pants like a clerk might, or someone who worked in a bank. He had a clipped moustache much like Mousey's. 'You were good,' Rafik said. 'You looked after him well.'

The man bowed his head. He knotted his hands behind his back.

'He was my brother and you cared for him.' Rafik took a crisp five-hundred-rupee note out of his wallet and then, on reflection, added another to it. 'He wasn't an easy man, I know. He had his ways. We grew up together after all.'

He remembered an Edh when they were boys, when they had named the bullocks, not understanding they were to be slaughtered. And on the morning of Edh, they had gone with their fathers to the field where the bullocks were kept. The animals were dressed with ornamental harnesses, with brightly coloured tassels and ropes of copper and gold. Rafik's bullock was slaughtered first. He was given the end of the harness to hold. When the blade began to saw through the animal's neck, it struggled, bucked, and kicked, dung and piss streamed between its legs, the violent movements wrenching the harness from Rafik's fingers. He turned to hide his face, but his father held him where he was, twisted him round by his shoulders so that his face was like a picture for all to see. Mousey took his hand, squeezed his fingers.

Rafik held the notes out to the man. The man dipped his head lower, kept his hands behind his back.

'Here,' Rafik said.

'Sahib,' the man said, 'Brother gave me enough, he gave me a lot, so much I cannot in a lifetime repay, and now, now there isn't time at all.' His shoulders shook.

It was an affront. The man must know, of course, what Mousey had written. He'd read the letter before giving it. Of course. Mousey hadn't any idea what they were like here,

these rogues. Rafik had a sudden monstrous vision of the
man standing over Mousey at his desk as he wrote. 'Don't be
foolish,' Rafik said, and tossed the money at him.

What would happen to Mousey's things, the man wanted
to know, his clothes, his books? He had cared very much for
books.

Had this man taken the clothes he was wearing from
Mousey's cupboard? They waited, these servants, barely a moment after a man had died, and then they rifled through his
things so that nothing was left, not even scraps for the crows.

It was all to stay as it was, Rafik said. Fahad might like
these things, he thought, this house even, Fahad might like it
for himself.

RAFIK JOINED SORAYA in Karachi for the wedding of the
son of a friend. The roads were blocked to all traffic but guests.
Cars were parked three, four deep. The chief of army staff was
expected to attend and on either side of the red-carpet entrance were rows of military guards standing to attention.

'A sad business,' Rafik said, meaning Mousey.

'The rat,' Soraya said, but without particular feeling. She
was in a white sari with strands of pearls to her waist, the
cloth tassel that tied the strands hanging down her bare back
between shoulder blades sharp and curved as scythes. She was
a column of light—quite unlike the other women who were
gaudily made-up, who glittered with gold and diamonds.

'The boy should come back,' he said.

'Hah,' she said. 'He'll want an apology first.'

'From?' he said.

'From you, of course.'

'Why?' He paused to shake the hand of a man who had approached him, and then another. 'From me?'

'You sent him away. He'll never return. This is what he says.'

Rafik told her about Mousey's letter and Mousey's conviction that the boy would come back. How long had it been?

'Now he's more from there than here,' she said. 'Fifteen years gone.'

A couple edged towards them. Glancing over, Soraya turned away. 'Ghastly,' she said. They hovered behind her shoulder awhile and then retreated into the crowd.

'A man is from where he is from,' Rafik said. 'They will never accept him there, the British.'

'Why are you telling me?' They wandered past the buffet tables, past a tempura station, past a sushi station, past a tandoor. 'You must be regretting it now,' she said. 'Everything you did.'

'I did? And you? You did nothing? Just chee, chee like a bird in a cage.' Some others wanted to greet him and he salaamed in their direction, before pivoting away. 'You put the idea in his head. London this, London that, the way that he would talk. Just like his mother.'

He introduced Soraya to the new French consul and his wife. They spoke briefly about an upcoming ball at the Club, about Gennifer Flowers, about the foreign exchange restrictions.

'I didn't tell him to leave the country,' Rafik continued, once they were alone again. 'He said that he would go. I only took him to Abad. I said, let him see the place. Let him understand. Should he sit in the house with women all his life?'

'He saw it and'—Soraya dusted her hands together—'that

was the end.' She laughed, that booming laugh that made everyone who was not looking already turn to stare.

'My little gadha,' he said, looping his arm round her waist.

'The donkey is you—' She jabbed him under his ribs with her elbow. A man preparing paan offered one to Soraya. She waved it away. He should make it afresh, she said. Less sweet, no betel nut.

Rafik mentioned what Mousey had asked of him, that he should give a hundred acres of land to one of the manservants.

'Of course,' Soraya said. 'This fellow and that.'

'I want him to come back,' Rafik said. 'The boy. My son should be here.'

'Then you bring him,' she said. 'You do nothing and expect everything done for you. Tell him. Or cut his allowance. Do something, even.' She pinched the freshly made paan between her nails, placed it delicately in her mouth. 'And you're alone. Of course this is what you're thinking. And all of them in Abad fleecing you, because they know you'll never see what's happening there, too busy going here and everywhere. Throwing this one in jail and that one. Soon there'll be no one left.'

In the distance, he spotted the governor and finance minister in conversation, the minister glancing across at Rafik and with a tilt of his head indicating that he should join them. If the boy came back, Rafik thought as he made his way towards them, he'd do Mousey that favour, as though it were a quid pro quo, as though one thing had anything to do with the other.

AT A TIME when talk of a coup became louder and Rafik should have stayed in the country, the PM engineered trips for him to Berlin, to Moscow, to London, to have him out of the way. Rafik would ordinarily have resisted, but London would be an opportunity to bring the boy back. He was certain enough of his position and there were others fighting his corner.

Since Mousey's death, there were moments when his mind became still as a pool and he could see his perfect reflection and he knew that he missed the boy, he wanted him around, he wanted the boy to see the things Rafik did, the most remarkable things, he wanted to tell the boy. He sent word through an official at the embassy in London who delivered the boy his monthly allowance that his father would be coming, that he had important things to say, and he told the official to give him twice as much as usual.

TWELVE

THE DAY RAFIK reached London, it was cool, there was a relentless rain fine as mist, and the light was so dim, it could have been early or late. But his mind was elsewhere, shuttling between generals and judges, senators and ministers. In Moscow, the Russian foreign minister had intimated he knew changes were afoot. 'When the cards are reshuffled,' he had said with a wink, 'the ace will come to the top, isn't that right?' And he had flashed his palm at Rafik.

Rafik had hurried through meetings in Berlin, had cut short his trip by a day, and now, arriving in London, he was disoriented, thinking Mousey was here, thinking Soraya and the boy were here together, reorienting himself only when his PA told him there were flood warnings for Abad, that his managers had called in a panic. Should they dig through the wall of the canal to release the water into the low-lying ground by the Baluchistan border?

'I can't be everywhere,' he'd told his PA. 'Idiots don't do what they're paid to. No sense at all.' If the boy were there, he could have taken charge. He was sharp, just a little sensitive—easily bruised. Abad would toughen him up. It was silliness that had kept him away so long.

On the way into the city from the airport, as he was passing Harrods, he directed the driver towards the flat, so that he could stop to say hello. It was only a little after sunrise—but what did the boy have to sleep in for, or wake up for? 'He can give me breakfast,' Rafik said to the driver, who nodded, averting his gaze.

'What more can he want,' Rafik said, 'what better location is there in the city than this?' And then, recognising the building, instructed the driver to stop.

White blossoms that had drifted from some nearby tree were scattered across the pavement, ground in places into a dirty yellow mulch that slipped against the soles of his shoes. Rubbish was littered across the steps to the basement flat and a half-eaten sandwich tossed into the stairwell.

Though the curtains were drawn in the window, Rafik rat-tatted against the pane. He crouched to pick up some mail that had spilled from the letterbox onto the doormat. The bell did not ring when he pressed it. He pressed again, then he knocked and waited, knocked and waited. He shouted up to the driver to ring at the main entrance to the building for the porter, explaining that the buzzer would be marked. After a short while, the driver called out to say that the porter had come.

Rafik found the man in slippers and a large shirt, its buttons askew. The zipper on his pants was undone and his hair was tousled. 'My son isn't answering,' Rafik said.

'It's only past six.' The porter frowned at him. 'The way you were shouting. People are sleeping.'

'Then he must be inside,' Rafik said, nodding towards the basement stairwell.

'Him? He's been gone months.' The porter pushed the door shut, disappearing behind it.

THE EMBASSY OFFICIAL confirmed this when Rafik sent for him later, the man twisting his head this way and that as though to look anywhere else but at Rafik. 'He said he was going somewhere,' the man said, waving as though that place were just here round the corner. 'I said, "You should take Sir's permission," and he gave an answer I won't repeat—children sometimes say these things. I said, "Sir has provided for you, has taken care of you, given you this beautiful apartment in the best location, best, best." He didn't want to take the money even. I said, "Your father will be angry with me if you don't, you must, you must." I put the envelope in his hand, then he took it. But he said, "Next time I won't," and the next time it was true, he did not.'

Then where was the money? Rafik said. 'You've been keeping it?' He slapped the man across the face. 'I expect you to watch after him and he goes and you say nothing? He stops taking his allowance and you say nothing? What is it? Do you have a brain?' Rafik rapped his knuckle against the side of his head. 'Can you think?'

He didn't have time to reflect further on these goings-on with the boy—there were meetings and functions throughout the days that followed, calls late into the night, and in the middle of it all, his manager called from Abad to report on the advancement of the flood-waters, which Rafik, with the assistance of the local military base, managed to divert onto the land of a neighbour who had ill-advisedly challenged him for his seat in the last election.

There were reports too that a reshuffle was now weeks away, that only one name—his—was being considered for the top spot. 'So change is afoot,' his British counterpart had said at a reception at the palace, 'and it seems you're the horse to bet on.'

There was a celebratory mood around him, as though the news had travelled. More than the usual number of bowers and scrapers flocked. For some reason, he imagined telling Mousey, and then, in his imagination, Mousey became the boy, and he imagined clapping him on the shoulder, hooking his arm around the boy's neck. 'We'll get you a plum post,' he imagined saying, 'whatever you want—the railways, a bank, a university to look after. I know you, you'll make a big success of it. I know, I know. All you have to do is come back.'

THE BOY WAS FOUND, of course. Those who made it their business to know knew all along where he was. He sent word that he'd meet his father, why should he have anything against it, but he wouldn't come to the embassy, or to the Dorchester, or to the flat. They could have dinner somewhere. He'd bring a friend.

He chose a restaurant in Mayfair. 'These boys,' Rafik said to the driver, as they made their way there, 'what can one do? Rascals.'

It was a famous place, the driver said, made to look like a ship inside, that famous ship that had sunk all those years ago. There was a film about it too.

It was on a street corner, with a doorman in a top hat to guide Rafik in, a pretty girl to take his jacket. He was the last to arrive, she said, guiding him down a wide curving staircase, into a bustling room with mirrored walls that made it appear like an endless warren, glittering and humming with figures.

'Pretty girl,' he said to her. 'Good work.'

She led him to a table. 'Oh, no,' he said, 'not this one.' He gave the boy's name again. He scanned the room but now the people at the table were standing, one pushing past a chair to greet him—garishly dressed, a gaudy silk shirt, rings in the ears and chains round the neck, hair like Liberace.

He waved his hand in Rafik's face, flapped it at Rafik. 'You're looking everywhere,' he said, 'but here.'

'Is it?' Rafik said, the figure in front of him resolving into a face that he recognised, that sharp nose, that petulant chin, the fragments reassembling into—it was—into the boy. 'Looking like somebody else. Completely different. All this. What is this?' Rafik laughed. 'Dressing up. Like a gigolo. But you should do what you want.'

The boy introduced his friend, a much older man, who was so heavy he struggled to stand and was breathless with the effort.

'Aaah,' Rafik said, resting his hand on the back of the chair that had been pulled out for him, studying the boy still, the boy's face shining so that it looked almost white, tight as a bladder. 'I'm only showing you,' Rafik said, gesturing at his own face so the boy should know what he meant, 'how a man should be. He should not appear vain.' But the boy would only look at his friend, dabbing at the corners of his lips with his napkin though there was no food on the table.

The friend invited him to sit, as though Rafik were attending at his invitation.

Rafik glanced around, glancing at the staircase that had brought him there. 'Your friend must take care of himself,' he said to the boy, sitting finally. 'Not good to have all this excess weight at his age.'

Menus were brought. He ordered Scotch, imagining Mousey in the empty seat across from him. 'Your uncle would have liked the place,' Rafik said.

The boy thrummed his fingers against the table, staring at his friend.

'You're seeing me after how long?' Rafik said.

The boy shrugged. 'Years,' he said.

'Too long for a father and son,' Rafik said. 'I told you about Mousey?'

The boy explained to his friend that Mousey was his father's cousin, that he'd lived in London and then returned to Abad and involved himself in the affairs of the farm.

'More English than the English,' Rafik said. 'A sad way to go.'

The boy jogged his knee so that the crystal and cutlery rattled. 'Don't do that,' Rafik said. Then, 'These silks, they go out of style very fast. A man shouldn't think of these fashions. He should dress so that what he wears today he can wear tomorrow. People should see the man, not the fashions. Isn't that right?' He directed this last question at the friend, who was soberly dressed, in a suit and tie, the buttons of his shirt straining across his belly. 'It's for you to decide,' he said to the boy. 'I only tell you what I think.' In a mirror across from where he sat, he watched a woman walk up the stairs to the exit, imagined his driver idling outside. 'Early flight tomorrow,' he said.

Rafik's drink arrived. 'My son enjoys these places,' he said in the direction of the friend. 'Always, he and his mother would come when he was a child, spend my money at places like this'—he gestured at the surrounding tables—'and shopping.' He looked at the boy again, though it was difficult for him, for some reason. 'Next time, I'll take you to Shezan on Montpelier Street. The food is excellent and they won't take a penny from us. They'll refuse. You go when you want. You take this man.' He gestured at the friend. 'You give them your name. They'll treat you like a king.'

The friend began speaking then—a voice reedy as a kazoo—talking endlessly about himself, what he did, about the global economy, about China.

'Yes, yes,' Rafik said, 'very good. Knows what he's saying.'

Their order was taken, the boy and his friend discussing at length this dish or that. 'It's all the same,' Rafik said. 'All a show, that's what it's about. I go from one function to the next and you see the same thing.'

'I like it,' the boy said, with that ugly, sullen expression on his face he would use as a child to get his way. He tugged a chain round his neck loose from his collar. He shook his wrist, shook the cuff of his shirt away.

'These are things your mother would wear,' Rafik said, gesturing at his bracelets. 'You tell him,' he said to the friend. 'You give him advice. He won't listen to his father. He just runs away.' He laughed.

Food was brought with great fanfare, plates turned just so, elaborate descriptions from the waitstaff of each one, the boy pointing at the dishes as though there were something remarkable in them.

'A clever boy doing nothing,' Rafik said. 'What a waste.

What a shame. He studied at the best schools. Has he told you? A man should have a profession.' If he came back to Pakistan, he could have any job he wanted, any job could be his. Rafik imagined saying this but did not. The words sat somewhere halfway up his chest and he swallowed them down. 'He could be anything, he could do anything,' he said instead.

The friend was talking about money now, how well he was doing, how he had revived businesses that were failing, how well he knew the Clintons.

'We have a number of businesses,' Rafik said. 'The cotton gins, the rice mills, a textile mill, a bank now—did I tell you this?'

No, the boy said, he hadn't. He wasn't doing nothing, he said, taking large gulps of his wine. 'You know that,' he said. 'I've told you many times.'

What was he doing then, Rafik wanted to know.

A book, the boy said. Writing a book.

'Very good,' Rafik said. 'Very, very good. But what do you have to write? This is something to do later in life. First at least a man should live. Isn't this right?' Rafik turned to the friend.

'I tell him to keep busy,' the friend said. 'To do something.'

'You see?' Rafik said. He found himself remembering Mousey again, remembering a meal he'd had with Mousey in London years ago, years and years ago. 'He left a letter,' Rafik said. 'He thought you would come back.'

'Come back where?' the boy said, frowning at the food on his plate.

'Where else?' Rafik said. 'Where else. Mousey wanted land to be given to some fellow. It's not something I can do.' He told this last part to the friend. 'Our custom is that land does not leave the family.'

LATER, IN THE BACK of the car on the way to his hotel, he thought of all the trouble Mousey had had coming back to Pakistan. 'Our people,' he told the driver, 'they come here and become more English than the English. Then they must stay. Isn't that so. How can they not.'

III

THIRTEEN

IT HAD BEEN a week of strange omens, like the distant rumblings before a storm. The wind whipped through the leaves, toppling bins, billowing raincoats, and upturning umbrellas. While Fahad was on his way to a class, a man had accosted him in the street. 'You have a lucky mark,' he'd said, pointing at Fahad's forehead. Fahad had slowed to nod a polite acknowledgement, at which point the man stopped him, insisting on reading his fortune from his palm. Fahad was distracted by the other pedestrians, thoughts of the class he was teaching. He was late. The man said something, repeated it, and then asked if Fahad had heard him. It was important. 'Did you hear? You didn't listen. Whose name begins with the letter M.' He'd traced the letter on Fahad's palm. 'Be careful.'

Fahad had gently withdrawn his hand and the man had asked for money. He was dressed like a clerk but wearing the turban and kara of a Sikh.

He didn't have any change, Fahad had said, patting his pockets demonstratively.

But the man wouldn't go away—tapping his own palm now, waving it in Fahad's face, thick and broad as a steak.

'I'm late,' Fahad said. 'I really have somewhere to be.'

And then the man imitated Fahad, made fun of the way he spoke and how he was dressed. He thought himself an Englishman but anyone could see, the man said. 'They can see from your face, brother, who you are, and you think you're the same as them.' He'd laughed a horrible laugh, curled his lips an ugly way, and then flicking his wrist at Fahad had spun away.

Fahad had quickly turned a corner and then another, stumbling into a wet mulch of leaves. Then, reminding himself again that he was late, he hurried to class.

THE NEXT EVENING, when he was leaving a restaurant on the Kings Road after dinner with friends, an old woman, smartly dressed in a jacket, a skirt, low heels, her hair set into firm curls, shoved Fahad with her fist and waved her cane at him. 'Go back to where you came from,' she said.

'People say that?' he'd asked Alex in shock when he got home.

IT MADE HIM think about the other place, about Abad, and memories of it still had the tenderness of a wound, even after thirty years away. He thought about the time before he left Abad, and then the country, the events that led to his departure, moments still so painful he could barely bring them to mind. But thoughts of Abad threaded through his other thoughts, so that buying groceries, plucking a jar of artichokes from a shelf, placing it upon the conveyor belt to pay, his own gestures began to seem exaggerated, as if he were playing a part. Then, during a workshop, an Indian student read aloud a village story she'd written, and when Fahad gave her feedback, he heard how much finer his consonants were than hers, that his t's and c's, sharp as blades, sliced through the front of his mouth while hers stirred from the well beneath her tongue. His voice had a falseness that hers did not, and when he spoke louder, as though that might give his voice strength, he heard himself become shrill.

In the student's story, a girl was raped in a field by an itinerant worker. The group discussed in detail how the student had choreographed the scene, and Fahad found himself remembering Abad again—the water thick as mud, the grey rocky earth, the dust that clouded up around you as you walked so that you appeared from it as if conjured by a sandstorm—but each thought shimmered both with warning and with poetry, luring him nearer like the dashing rocks of the Symplegades. What if, he wondered, for a terrible moment, he'd written nothing in so long because he hadn't written this, because he'd written always so far away from himself, as though tossing a grenade?

HE AND ALEX had invited friends for lunch at theirs that Sunday. It was blustery and though there was no rain, pebbles and earth scattered against the pane. Something that had come loose from somewhere banged outside.

As Alex cleared the soup bowls, Fahad told the story about the man who had accosted him on that unprepossessing stretch of Cromwell Road. He did not tell the group that the man was Sikh, nor what he had said after Fahad had refused to tip him, telling them only that he became irate.

'And M,' a friend asked, 'who in the world could that be?' They guessed: an ex of Fahad's, an old college friend, a troublesome neighbour.

'Mousey,' Fahad said, surprising himself, and then wondering whether he could explain who Mousey was.

He told Mousey's story, that he'd spent all those years *here* of all places, in an apartment on Cadogan Square, that he had a thing for suits from Huntsman and shoes from Lobb, a regular table at Mirabelle.

'It runs in the family,' someone said, laughing, edging out of the way so that Alex could set the stew down, a dish of baked endives, a salad of wild dandelion.

And then Mousey had come back, Fahad continued, hurrying a little, as though he were afraid if he paused a moment, he might remember that he couldn't think of this at all.

Mousey's father had died. The father was an old rogue, born into power, a cabinet minister and all that for many years, a people's person, hugely popular though who knew why—and he couldn't stand his son.

It was beef daube, Alex explained, lifting the lid away, a fug of steam rising from the pan.

Mousey returned to Pakistan, took over his father's land, a sizeable farm, a few thousand acres. 'He had all sorts of ideas, to go organic, to mechanise everything, to build schools and health centres in every village.'

Had Alex met him? someone asked.

Mousey died years ago, Fahad said. 'Alex hasn't even met my parents.'

'Another lifetime,' Alex said.

Fahad should write about it, someone said. It was like something out of Tolstoy.

'It is.' Fahad refilled his own glass. But Mousey didn't speak the language, he didn't know a soul, he hired a handsome young estate manager—'That really does run in the family,' someone said, and this time everyone laughed—and poured money into his projects, but none of it went anywhere. The tillers tied him up in knots, ran circles around him, told him high land was low and low land was so poor it should be sold for pennies. His schools were used as gathering places for the village elders and the health centres were shelters for goats. His teachers were co-opted into other work. Finally, his crops failed for lack of water. And then, then he just gave up.

Fahad found himself breathless, as though the story were a boulder he'd chased down a hill, his father at the very bottom.

'A sad story,' someone said.

'Just as well—you saved yourself.' Alex squeezed Fahad's shoulder as he passed.

'Yes,' Fahad said, wondering why he had left his own father out of Mousey's story, when his father had been such a part of it. Fahad's father didn't need defending. He didn't even need thinking about.

The conversation had moved on to holidays, to Italy. Venice was sinking. Someone said, 'We should go again before it's gone.'

'But is it really?' Fahad said. It began to rain.

LATER, IN BED, the wind thudding against the walls, Fahad said, 'Don't you wonder about it? A whole part of my life—'

'What you left behind,' Alex said, reaching across the comforter to Fahad, their hands not quite touching. The wind howled. Was the beef a little dry? Alex wondered aloud. The oven was so unpredictable. He'd order a thermometer.

Fahad thought of Alex's mother—who had barely recognised them the last time they visited—of the house Alex had grown up in, which he'd sold once she was in care. 'Do you think about your father, what he would have been like?'

'How could I know?' Alex said. 'It's like asking about a life I never had.'

'Yes,' Fahad said, going back to his book, though he wasn't reading it, turning the page, though he'd have to turn back.

'I could feel sad,' Alex said. 'You can always feel sad, if you want. Or I could be here.' He patted the comforter.

It had been a Georgian terraced house in a smart suburb of Bath, cluttered with decades of photographs and knick-knacks, china figurines on the mantel, an ornamental bird-cage, lamps with frilled lampshades. Alex had wanted nothing from there. He'd taken what was his when he moved out, he said. 'It's things.' He shrugged at a porcelain jug in the shape of a cow. He glanced around. 'Walls. A floor. A staircase.' They didn't linger.

He was snoring softly now, an island on the far side of their enormous bed. Fahad switched off his bedside light. He felt for Alex's cool fingers, linking his into them.

THE FOLLOWING WEEKEND, Alex was watching something on TV while Fahad was at the kitchen table reading student assignments. Alex tilted his head to one side. 'Your phone,' he said. 'Isn't it ringing?' He turned the volume of the TV down. After a moment, Fahad heard it. 'It's been going awhile,' Alex added, turning the volume up again.

Fahad's phone was in the bedroom, half off the edge of the bedside table. It had stopped ringing but as he picked it up, it began again, the first few digits of the dialling code for Pakistan flashing on the screen, and he tossed the phone onto the bed, turned it facedown, and watched it vibrate.

'You can't find it?' Alex called out from the living room, his voice modulating as though he might have stood up from the sofa, on his way to help.

'Found it,' Fahad shouted. It stopped ringing. Then, it started again, and this time he answered.

'Hello?'

'Hello?' he said.

'Is it you?' a woman's voice said.

'Hello?' he said again.

'Fahad? Is that you?' It was his mother.

Yes, he said. Was everything alright?

It wasn't that she never called, only that they had developed a routine over these years of speaking only on birthdays: brief conversations, briefer than the message you'd write in a card, usually only the two of them. He'd tell her to wish his father from him or she'd tell him his father sent his wishes, but once or twice, he'd spoken to his father too.

'I've called and called,' she said. What was the sense of these new mobile phones if he didn't carry it with him?

'I was in the other room,' he said. 'I was working.' He hadn't been expecting a call, he added. He tried to avoid being disturbed while he was working.

'Is it alright?' she said. 'Is it alright, is it alright.' There was a thud and distortion, as though she had dropped the receiver, muffled voices, and then her again, 'No, no, no, no. It's too much now, it's too much. I should just throw myself down the stairs. If we had any stairs.'

A letter had come, God knows when, it had been lying some days in his father's study, but why had the servants left it there. 'They don't think, they don't have brains, or they want to cause trouble, it will be trouble for them, that's what it will be.' Her voice was ragged.

The letter was from the court. It could have been there for weeks. It could have disappeared. And then what would have happened?

But what had happened? he asked.

His father had ruined them, that was what, she said. 'Thrown out of my own house, imagine that.'

'Out of the house?' he said. 'Why would you be thrown out of the house? What do you mean ruined?' He glanced down the hallway. Alex was still in the living room. Fahad grabbed a jacket and slipped out of the front door. 'Maybe you're confused,' he said, thinking of Alex's mother, how easily she panicked, how little she seemed to understand.

'Ruined,' she said again, this time even more desperately. 'Why did he trust these people?' she said. 'I blame him, I do, even if he doesn't know, even if his mind is half gone.'

It was stormy outside, and the wind, wet with rain, snatched at her voice as she spoke, stealing a word here, a word there.

His father had borrowed against the house in Karachi, he'd borrowed against everything, but why this house? 'Must we lose everything?' she said. 'I'll wear old clothes, I'll go without a car, with barely any staff, I won't travel, I'll sell the jewellery my mother gave me, but a roof over my head, how can I do without that?'

He found himself by the railings outside the Natural History Museum, gripping them as though he might blow away like the leaves whirling up round his legs. Why had he borrowed? Fahad asked.

He'd spent so much on the elections and after he lost, he'd spent more the next time, and the next, but those days were over, she'd told him that, the days of gentlemen in the Assembly, now they were all thugs and crooks, buying votes and paying bribes and holding judges hostage. And why had he taken on the generals, thinking he was tougher than all of them? 'One day, there's a lion bigger,' his mother said. 'And he makes mincemeat of you.'

'But the mills,' Fahad said, 'aren't they making money?'

'The mills?' His mother laughed. 'They're long gone,' she said, sold to pay off other debts. He'd always trusted the wrong people, she said. Left them to run this business and that. They'd ask for money and he'd send it. They'd ask him to sign one document or another and he'd do it without thinking, without looking. 'He thought no one could touch him,' she said. 'And now look. Now see. Who is there even? You lose your position, and everyone forgets who you are. There was a time they said he'd be PM and there were crowds, you'd never seen so many—from the front door of this house here in Karachi all the way to Frere Hall. Where are they now?'

It didn't make sense to him. 'It doesn't make sense,' he

said. 'The mills are gone? What about Abad?' Even the name of the place made something twist through his stomach.

'Abad? They take money—they don't send it from there,' she said. 'His managers calling every month asking for millions to buy this or that,' and then, after a strange pause, the line crackling, she added, 'but maybe it can save us.'

'What do you mean?' he said. 'When did it happen?'

'I'm telling you,' she said, 'I just saw the letter now. I don't know when it came.'

'Not the letter, but all this, these loans and the mills closing.'

'Yes,' she said. 'The wolves have been at the door so many years now. I forget what it was like before. To not toss and turn with worry every night. I forget.'

A woman was standing at the top of the steps in front of the museum, her features fixed in an odd expression, the wind whipping her hair around her face. A gust swiped a pamphlet from under her arm, tossed it a distance away. She flailed out, hurried down the steps after it, but now it spun up into the air again.

'Are you alright?' Fahad said, wondering at once if any of what his mother had said was true. What if it wasn't? He could speak to his father, he thought, though he never did. He could speak to one of the servants.

'Are you listening?' she said. 'We'll be thrown out onto the street in weeks. This is what the letter says. They'll take the house. I've done what I can all this time. Now I can't. I can't.' She said this last part more insistently, as though he were disagreeing.

A bus stopped, an alarm sounded, and a platform extended from beneath its doors like a tongue. It was absurd and at once everything was absurd: the tourists huddling by the gates to the museum, a pair of pigeons pecking at a plastic bag, an elderly man pushing an empty pram diagonally across the road despite the oncoming traffic. How grey it was, how grey, as if there were no such thing as sun.

His mother was talking still. Why had his father never trusted family, she was saying. Never her, never Fahad, never even that cousin of his, who for all his faults, for all his ugly habits, was not a thief. 'The ones who are close,' his mother said, 'he doesn't notice us. Always making a fuss of others. Well look what they have done now.'

Where was he? Fahad asked, meaning his father.

'You're not hearing,' his mother said. 'He's gone in the mind. Sometimes he thinks I am somebody else. Sometimes he walks in the night down the street till they stop him, the guards outside the corps commander's house, or some rehri wallah.'

Fahad held the phone at a distance. Her voice became cartoonishly small. It seemed to him that all he had to do was hang up and this would disappear.

If there was anyone else, God knows, she'd ask, his mother was saying. Hadn't she already? Begged from door to door like a refugee, asking this old friend and that to speak to a judge, to speak to a general, to speak to a minister.

But the letter had come today, he asked.

Who knows when it came, she said, how long it was sitting on the desk in his father's study.

'There must be someone who can help,' he said, trying to think of the names of his parents' friends and acquaintances and failing.

'What can anyone do?' She sounded almost hysterical now, her voice warbling as though she had no control of it. There was only one thing to do. 'Nothing left to do but this,' she said. 'And? If it kills your father? You think I haven't thought? You think I haven't prayed? I, who never pray, even that I have done, I have joined my hands and bowed my head, even that. And still, there is only this to do.'

He did not want to know what it was, this last resort. What was it to do with him? Did she want money, money from him? Something about that idea gave him a discomfiting thrill. 'If I could help, of course I would,' he said, 'but—'

'There's no one else,' she said. 'It must be you. I cannot. If your father understood, he would not do it. So then?'

'I made some money from the first book,' he said, not wanting her to think he hadn't, he had, after all, he had, 'but that was years ago. It's been years now.'

'Not money. You keep your money,' she said. 'Abad.'

What did she want? Did she want him to manage the farm? 'My work is here,' he said, 'or I'd do something.'

'A few weeks off they'll give you,' she said. 'If you tell them, these people you work for. Of course they will.'

An alarm began ringing. The headlights on a parked car a short distance ahead were flashing. He was on a street he didn't recognise. Which way had he come?

'At some point,' he said. 'It's a busy time.'

Again, there was the sound of scrabbling, she called out to someone, he couldn't make out the words. 'You're not hearing,' she said. Unless the farm was sold, how could they repay the loan? And if the loan wasn't paid, the house would be taken from over their heads, the ground from under them.

There was a man who was interested in buying Abad, a man who kept calling.

'Sold?' he said.

It was dark by the time he returned to their mansion block. The lights had not yet been switched on inside the hallway. He took the stairs, each step somehow an impossible effort. He glanced again at his phone, to be sure that she had called, and there it was, that incomprehensibly long number on the bright screen. To go back, to go back for this, the idea was impossible. It was all impossible, impossible that any of it had happened at all. And yet, his father's ruin, if it had happened like this, began, as he neared the front door of their apartment, to seem almost inevitable.

He was grateful, now more than ever, that Alex took no interest, that Alex was as far away from Fahad's family, from the house in Karachi, from Abad, as it was possible to be. From the foyer, Fahad could see the back of his head. He was in front of the TV still. Fahad closed the door softly. In their bedroom, he stood awhile by the bed. Then, he riffled through the drawers on his side of the cupboard. A light from somewhere played in ripples across the cupboard doors when he shut them, and he thought of the farm, of the dappled sunlight on a forest floor, of a wind chime ringing, of bright shards of mirrored glass swaying on threads in a window-like opening, of something shifting in the undergrowth, a feeling crackling through the air like a current.

'Did you go somewhere?' It was Alex, switching on the bedside lamps. 'I heard the door, I thought.' He put his hand on Fahad's back. 'What's that?' He took from Fahad's hand the passport Fahad had found in his drawer.

His mother had called, Fahad said, unable to stop himself, unable to think of anything else to say, and why not say it? They were having troubles, his parents. His father, she said, wasn't so well.

'They get older.' Alex followed him to the bathroom.

Fahad shook his head, shrugged. 'I won't go back,' he said. He turned the tap on. He washed his hands. 'I won't go.'

'You don't have to,' Alex said.

In the mirror, the two of them, they looked like strangers: Fahad's skin so sallow and Alex with his paunch and shock of dull, grey hair.

REMEMBERING WHAT his mother had told him that night as he lay unsleeping in bed, then the next day on the way to class, and at class, he didn't believe it, he didn't, but then he pictured his parents in rags, the house crumbling around them, their faces grimy with dust. As he replayed in his mind the things she'd said, her words and her phrases had the sharpness of deceit, of cunning even, but, as he remembered them, sometimes the words wavered uncertainly, sometimes they strained with worry.

What if it was true? Would he go? They could clap their hands and send him away as a boy of barely sixteen, because he didn't suit their purposes, because he interfered with their ambitions, and clap them again all these years later and expect him to return? The feelings he'd had in those earlier years in London, of rage, of wanting to punish his parents one day as they'd punished him, he'd conquered them, he thought, but now he felt a premonition of their return.

SOMETIMES TOO, he felt something like yearning, something like nostalgia. 'You don't even know the place,' he told himself. 'You aren't remembering, you're imagining.' Whatever it was, it had a force that tugged at him and he found himself, at odd moments, conjuring little scenes: the gardens at Frere Hall, Jehangir Kothari Parade at Seaview, the air gritty with salt, rain in the courtyard of the house. Scenes from Abad too, the name no longer startling him when he sounded it out in his head: buffalo wallowing in the canal, the water bronze with silt, the sky the colour of dust, the hot, hot sun that for some reason could never be seen.

HE CALLED THE HOUSE in Karachi again, calling when it would be the middle of the day, in the hope his parents would be napping, that perhaps one of the servants would answer. It was a man whose voice he didn't recognise and having to speak suddenly in Urdu, the words were like stones in his mouth.

Everyone is resting, the man said abruptly. You should call another time.

'Where is Ayah?' Fahad asked.

'I don't know where she is.'

'Call her,' Fahad said. 'Tell her it's—tell her it's the Little Sir.'

The man's footsteps became faint. The phone had been on a teak bar in the courtyard. The ceiling had been a grid

of skylights and Fahad imagined the space colonnaded with
light from the late-afternoon sun, water plashing in the
sunken fountain in the centre, his parents' room icy cold, dark
and still as a mausoleum. The afternoon there had an intersti-
tial quality, time endlessly suspended.

'Baba?' It was old Ayah—shrill as a bird. 'What a thing it
is,' she said. 'I prayed and prayed for you. Your parents are
resting. Your father, he's awake through the night, walking
and walking, sometimes outside the house, sometimes out
into the road. Sometimes he doesn't know who it is, even
where. If you stop him, he becomes angry. Once he pushed
me so hard I fell. Of course I say nothing. It's your father
after all. We're his children. We eat the salt from his table.
Your mother didn't want to trouble you. I was the one, I said,
"Baba will fix this. He will help you." And your mother, she
cries alone in her dressing room. She thinks no one can hear,
but from the passage outside, I hear everything. I said, "If you
ask him, he will never say no, never to you. He's a good boy."'

The words surfaced in his mind a memory of leaving that
house for the last time, pausing at the threshold, his case
by his side, refusing in that moment to look back, gripping
the handle of that case so tightly that his nails left half-moons
at the edge of his palm.

'It's a duty, isn't it,' she continued, 'for one to help another, for a child to help his parents.'

He felt at once like a child, the boy who had been sent
away.

'What all they have done,' he said.

'Yes?' she said. 'You'll make it better. I know you will.'

'Your father,' she continued, 'I weep when I see him. He
walks and he walks but he goes nowhere, he sees no one.

He hasn't been to the farm in more than a year. You come, you take him there with you. That is his home more than here even. His heart is there.'

The day Fahad had left Karachi, his father had patted him on the back, still refusing to look him in the eye. 'Better there,' his father had said. 'Good boy. Good, good. All for the best.'

Sell the farm, yes, he'd do it.

FOURTEEN

WHEN RAFIK AND MOUSEY were boys, they'd carry charpayees to the roof, where it was cooler, where they might
sometimes find a breeze to tickle the soles of their feet, their
ears, the insides of their elbows, the moon and stars bright
enough for Mousey to lie on his stomach and read. Sometimes, he'd read aloud. Sometimes, he'd say strange things,
about this manservant or that, what this one did, or how that
one looked, or how that one looked at him, how the driver
bounced him on his lap.

Rafik would tell him, 'Leave it. What is it to talk
about?'

Sometimes, when it was too hot to sleep, when there was
no breeze at all, the air still and dry as dirt, they'd look in
the night sky for the stars they knew, this galaxy or that: the
one shaped like a bowl, the one that was the hunter. Mousey
knew them all. And this one here, shaped like a scythe, which
was this? Mousey, which one was this?

But he wasn't on the roof, he was in the house and there
was a great commotion. 'Is there a wedding?' Rafik asked

Ayah, who was banging pots in the kitchen, now dragging a bench nearer the kitchen counter, clambering up and disappearing into a cupboard. The bearer was in the guest room at the top of a tall ladder, piles of bedding on the bed, a comforter in a heap on the carpet.

'All this mess,' Rafik said.

Outside, the driver was polishing the bonnet of the car with a rag.

Soraya was at the table in the courtyard, the newspapers spread open in front of her to the crosswords. She looked up in his direction in a blank, unseeing sort of way.

'So much commotion,' Rafik said. 'Is there a wedding?'

'Again they found you on the driveway in the night,' she said, tucking with the nib end of her pen a wayward curl behind her ear. 'Where were you going?'

'In the night?' he said.

'Barefoot, in your pyjamas, with your suitcase.'

'My case?'

'Taking only a pair of shoes in it, nothing else.'

He glanced over the crossword, at half an entry she had crossed out.

'And you wouldn't come in,' she continued, 'fighting with them.' She sat forward suddenly and scribbled something across the page.

The bearer appeared from the end of the hallway, a bedsheet spread open between his arms, a tear from corner to corner. There wasn't a matching set, he said.

'Not one?' she said. 'How can that be?'

'They take everything,' Rafik said. 'Back to their quarters. All of them living here, children, grandchildren, great-grandchildren.'

The bearer pinned that sheet between his knees and held out another for Soraya's approval.

'Is someone coming?' Rafik said.

Now it was Ayah from round the fountain, with a tray, with a bowl with something floating in it. 'See,' she said, 'what I found in the freezer, at the bottom.' She tilted the tray and the bowl slid along it. 'A chicken. I'll roast this, with potatoes. Baba likes potatoes.'

'Very good,' Soraya said.

'But after this, there's nothing,' Ayah said. 'Not even an onion. Only the box soup. And even that, only three boxes and one of those I'm bringing you now for lunch.'

She returned after a time with two mugs of soup and a large steaming dish of rice.

'This is the world's staple,' Rafik said, spooning rice into his mug, stirring the contents. 'This is all a man needs.'

'Now don't cause trouble,' Soraya said, holding a spoon up to her lips, pursing her lips, 'or no one will help us.'

'Trouble?' Rafik said. 'Nobody's causing trouble.'

'Why didn't he come all these years?' Soraya said. 'He didn't want to. He says, "You sent me away." He says, "I was banished." This is what is in his head.'

'No, no,' Rafik said. 'He'll come and he'll stay.'

'He won't stay, but he can do something. How can I alone? I can't anymore. And all these things, these things are falling on top of us'—she looked up as though they might fall now—'and I, I am finished too.' She jittered her fingernail against the table.

'I'll tell him,' Rafik said, 'his land is here. Who will manage it? He must come and do it himself. I'll help him, of course. I'll show him how.'

'What interest will he have in the land?' she said. 'London is his home now, through and through. That was the mistake, for him to go there in the first place.'

'No, he must,' Rafik said. 'Or what will happen to Abad? I can help. I'll tell him that. I'll tell him, "I'll help, but this land is yours. Now you must manage it."'

'You just don't make trouble,' Soraya said. 'That's all.'

'Don't I want him to stay?' He tugged the dish of rice nearer him. 'It tastes of nothing,' he said of the soup. 'Even water has a taste, but not this. And what are these pieces?' He showed her a scrap on the tip of his tongue.

'Something,' she said. 'A vegetable. A carrot.'

'He's not like his father,' Rafik said. 'His father was a different kind of man. People loved him. He drank and drank, but they loved him. You couldn't find him alone one moment of the day. Even when he went to the washroom. He left his land to me, he said, "You manage all this. My son doesn't care a damn. He'll never come back." "He'll come," I said. And now, you see.'

'Who are you saying?' Soraya said. 'It's Fahad. You remember? Fahad is coming.'

The wind chimes by the doors to the terrace tinkled.

'Yes,' Rafik said. 'Fahad.'

Soraya called out for Ayah and then, when the old woman came hurrying again, Soraya gave some instruction, tapping the edge of the rice dish, tapping the side of her mug.

'He's coming after how long?' Rafik said.

'Many years,' Soraya said. 'How long? Since he was a boy.'

'He's older now,' Rafik said.

'Much older.'

'What does he do,' Rafik said, 'over there?'

'Please'—she raised her hand, as if to halt him—'you just be calm, be pleasant.'

'I'm very calm,' Rafik said. 'Why shouldn't I be calm?'

'I'm tired,' Soraya said. 'I can't anymore. I'm too tired, please—' She joined her hands as if in prayer.

Their mugs were cleared but Rafik held on to the rim of the rice dish so that it couldn't be removed.

'He's writing these books,' Soraya said. 'It's here on this shelf.' She gestured towards their bedroom. 'And some other things. It's up to him to decide.'

'Of course it's up to him,' Rafik said. 'It's a shame, he's a clever boy.' Above a jali panel of the gridded roof of the courtyard, birds fluttered their wings at each other.

'He must be doing alright,' she continued. 'He isn't asking for money anymore.'

'This one at the Club was saying that I should write a book myself,' Rafik said.

Soraya shouted out some other instruction to the bearer now, called his name once, and then again.

'"You," he said to me, it was this one, the brother of your friend, you remember?' he said. '"You are a library, you are a library," he said, "because you were there"'—Rafik knocked on the table—'"history is being made of this country and you are there, like a camera. No, more than a camera. Because you are making the history." This is what he said. He said, "It is your duty, your duty," he said, "to write the record because the record is for everyone. For you to say, this happened and this happened and this happened. I know because, one, I saw it, two, I did it. This is your duty," he said. "I'm not interested in these things," I said to him. "Some men want a statue, they want an airport with their name. I'm a humble man," I said. "It is not a question of interest. It is your duty." This is what he said. "I don't have the time," I said. "I'm not this kind of person. There is the person who does the thing and the person who writes the thing. I am the one doing."' Rafik knocked the table again. 'But I kept all the files, every letter, everything. The record is there. It needs only to be—' He gestured with pinched fingers as though he were scribbling.

But Soraya had risen and was halfway across the courtyard.

Somehow, from that distance she saw enough to call out, 'Where are you taking my rice?'

'You've eaten,' he said. 'You've got up and you've gone away.'

'Please,' she said, signalling to Ayah to wait, hurrying back towards Rafik, 'the cupboards are bare. I promise you, the birds will eat very well without you.'

But he was already at the sliding doors that led onto the terrace, the dish of rice balanced across his forearm. 'How little they are and how big you are,' he said. 'To them you are a giant.'

'Then take only so much.' She made the shape of a mouthful with her fingers.

THE BIRDS HAD already gathered in anticipation. If it had been anyone else approaching, they would have darted away, but they knew him well enough—even the sparrows, even the mynahs hopped nearer. He scraped the entire dish of rice

into an earthenware platter in the centre of the terrace so
that it became a giant mound, so that grains spilled out onto
the rough sandstone tiles.

'You, of course,' he said, addressing the two large crows,
one at the rim of a plant pot, the other in the champa, at the
end of a slender branch, which bowed under its weight. 'You
hold on,' and he shooed at them, pivoting so that he was in
their way, to allow the smaller birds to hop nearer, to peck at
the grains that had fallen.

'He's coming,' he said to the birds. 'After a long time he's
coming.' The gesture he made frightened them back and so
he became still again. 'It's good,' he said.

THE BEARER WAS beating a carpet outside on the driveway,
his head hovering above a cloud of dust. 'For the Little Sir,'
he said when Rafik asked.

'He's coming to stay,' Rafik said. 'Then you'll see. He'll fix
you all. I'm too easy, he'll say. I let you get away with murder.

'He's writing books,' Rafik continued. 'He'll write a book
for me.' The dust rose up around the man till he disappeared
entirely. 'Books matter. You teach your children to read,'
Rafik said. 'You send them to school. I'll give you the money.'

'They go to school,' the man said. He had a large paddle
and swung it in an arc high above his head.

'All my files,' Rafik said, 'I kept every record, every receipt.
It should be in a museum. You know what a museum is?'

The dust wasn't good to breathe, the man said, Sahib
shouldn't stand so near. It would go to his chest.

'I know what's good and what isn't,' Rafik said. Now,
where was the key to his office? Everything was there. He'd

kept it all in perfect order. The baba would want to see. 'He'll find it very interesting,' Rafik said.

The key was brought. The windows were cloudy with dirt. Inside, there was a thick layer of grime over the desk and the old computer his assistants had never used, all of them for some reason preferring instead to write by hand or on a typewriter, which was now nowhere to be found. For a moment, he heard the keys clacking, saw that old white-haired fellow of his, the one with the moustache, the one who had died so young, glancing up from his work.

The files were neatly shelved, each one dated, some marked with the names of places or people. Here was the OIC Summit, here was the visit of Rajiv Gandhi, each one had an index at the front, dividers, envelopes of photographs, a letter here, a memorandum there, the minutes of a meeting. The boy would be astonished. Who kept records like this? It was an archive of the history of the country. 'Of my part,' Rafik said aloud.

He arranged the files on the desk in stacks. He pushed the computer aside, wrenching at its cables to tug them out of the way, the cables twisting round his wrists, binding his hands together somehow—and then he woke with his face stuck to a plastic envelope, pain spiking through his neck as he peeled his cheek away, someone silhouetted through the open door of the office.

'The Little Sir has arrived.' It was the bearer. 'They're sitting to lunch.'

'But we had lunch only now,' Rafik said, turning his wrist towards himself, as though he were wearing a watch.

THE TABLE WAS SET in the dining room. Someone was sitting in Rafik's place. He had glossy hair streaked with white and high as a helmet and his head was bent over a plate, although he glanced at Soraya now and again, saying things Rafik couldn't hear from the hallway over the whirr of the air conditioner.

'Who is this?' Rafik said, sliding the glass door open. 'Look,' he said to Soraya, 'who this is. Almost as white as mine, his hair.' Rafik clapped him on the shoulder. 'My boy,' he said. 'Isn't that who it is? Isn't it? Hmm?'

The boy made as if to stand but did not. 'No, no,' Rafik said. 'Sitting in my place, you rascal. Sit, sit. What have I been doing? I've been busy for you. Yes, for you. Preparing papers. Things you'll find of great interest. You will be amazed when I show you. Things you've never seen before.

'You're like a stranger here,' he added. And then to Soraya, 'Isn't that how he seems? But doesn't he look like this one? This one who's gone? Carbon copy.'

'Let him talk,' Soraya said.

'Who's stopping him?' Rafik said. 'Take, take, this is all for you.' He crowded the dishes on the table towards the boy, a roast chicken, potatoes the size of fists. 'What do we eat? Soup only, lunch and dinner. Sometimes not even dinner.'

Rafik asked him how his journey had been. 'It's like he's always been here, isn't it?' he said to Soraya.

The boy spoke a little about his flight, the weather in London, how cold it had been, how unprepared he was for this heat. He hooked a finger inside the placket of his shirt and shook it loose. His face was as sharp as Soraya's, his eyes were as sunken and watchful as hers, looking as though he might at any moment dart away, disappear.

And what did he think of the place, Rafik asked, gesturing around them. How did he find it and them? 'He eats like you,' Rafik said, 'this careful way—' And he showed how the boy moved his lips like a bird.

'He's won awards,' Soraya said, 'he was just saying some award from the Netherlands.'

'Very good,' Rafik said. 'These things count for something.' There was a book of his here, wasn't there, Rafik said. 'What you've done we've kept carefully. We have it all on the shelf.'

The boy spoke barely at all. 'Still he doesn't talk,' Rafik said. 'How much commotion there's been in the house. Everyone asking when will he come, everyone busy, in the kitchen, in the rooms, the driver with the car.'

But as before the boy had an appetite, taking a great interest in what was in this dish, what was in that. 'You'll find it most interesting what I'm going to show you,' Rafik said. 'People are telling me all the time, they're saying, "Not a question of if but must. You *must* make the record. Put on record. You are not a witness but a, a, what's the word, you are sitting there at the very table." This is what people are saying. But I say, "Only one person can write this book and that is who? My son."' He reached across the table towards Fahad. '"I will allow no one else," I say. Afterwards I'll show you. Everything is kept so that anything can be found. Each file with an index at the front. They don't know here how to keep records, but I showed them. I know how important it is.'

'You should set the record straight,' Soraya said. 'People forget. They say all kinds of things.'

'Yes,' Rafik said. 'What things?'

She shouted out for more rotis, for more roast potatoes.

'Once it is written,' Rafik said, 'once it is history, no one can question it.'

Dishes were brought, and Ayah, fussing and crying, set them out in front of the boy like an offering.

'Just leave the food and no fuss,' Rafik said. 'Look at this fuss.'

'He's come,' Ayah said. 'It will be better now,' and then began to cry again.

'Shoo,' Rafik said. 'Go, go.'

The boy dug a spoon into the dish of potatoes.

'He wants to go to Abad,' Soraya said.

'Very good,' Rafik said. 'Abad is the place,' he continued, 'that has given us everything.' He spread his arms out to encompass the house. 'The goose that laid the golden egg.'

Soraya had sent for the phone and now the bearer brought the receiver, whipping the cord behind him to turn the corner that led into the room.

'You came with me,' Rafik said. 'You remember? To Abad. You didn't want to leave. You said, "This place is not *a* home, it is *the* home." You said, "How can we help these people. We should help them. They have too little." I said, "They have more than you can see. They're sharper than you and I put together." And who was right?'

Soraya spoke into the receiver and then held it towards Rafik. 'I've told them you're coming,' she said.

'He's looking like a gentleman,' Rafik said, gesturing at the boy, 'isn't he? But too much like a stranger.' He held up his fingers, pinching them together with his thumb. 'The flavour is in here. Leave all this.' He collected the cutlery from around the boy's plate. 'Eat with your hand.'

Soraya shook the receiver at Rafik till he took it.

'Yes, yes,' he said, and instructed the man on the other end to do as Soraya had requested.

'So?' Rafik said to the boy, who bent his head low over his plate. 'You're alright for money?'

The boy frowned and looked at his mother.

'Tell me, I'm asking you, not your mother,' Rafik said.

The boy nodded that he was.

'And you're busy?'

The boy nodded again.

'But a home is a home,' Rafik said. 'You come, you go, but this'—and he pointed emphatically down—'it has a feeling that no other place does. Why? Because you don't have to think, do I do this, do I do that, you just know what you do.'

'He's here a week,' Soraya said. 'Then back to London.'

The boy made some excuse about why he had to leave so soon, peering again into the dishes on the table, spooning dal onto his plate, bhindi, another potato.

AFTER THE MEAL had been cleared, Rafik suggested the men retire to his study, where, he winked in Soraya's direction, they could talk in peace. But the boy was tired, he'd travelled through the night. 'Of course, of course,' Rafik said. 'Of course.'

Still, rather than nap, Rafik had his files brought to his study. He flicked through them, smoothing the pages that had folded over and creased. 'It's funny,' he said, 'that of all things, paper can have the most value.' And it was what the boy was doing with his own life, he'd remember to tell him that. 'You're doing this yourself. Everything in paper.'

It was a strange thing, seeing this man in the house, this man who was his son. During lunch he had had to remind himself that Fahad was here. It had seemed for a moment that the man was someone else, some other visitor.

When the room became dim, Rafik wandered around the house. He found the cook sitting on a bench in the kitchen, fanning herself with a folded newspaper. 'God has answered our prayers,' she said.

'Not the crying,' Rafik said. 'Not this drama again.'

'But he has come back—' She dabbed at her face with the corner of her sari. 'I showed him all the old pictures I kept. When this one came to the house, when that one sang right here in the courtyard and we danced, all of us even, my son and daughter, my grandchildren weren't yet born, and I carried the Little Sir in my arms and danced with him. He laughed and laughed when I told him the old stories. Now he's gone to see the washerman and the others.' She nodded towards the servants' quarters.

Rafik looked from the end of the driveway where the yard began but between the servants' lean-tos and the sheets hung out to dry he could only see a tethered goat, somebody's puppy.

'Whose dog is it?' he said to the cook. 'Who gave permission for a dog?'

'You did,' she said. 'My grandson showed you, and you gave even the name.'

'It's as though this house belongs to the world,' he said. 'Everyone does what they want.'

BUT THE BOY did come later to find Rafik in the study. Why was he sitting in the dark, the boy wanted to know, reaching over to switch on the lamp.

Once the boy was there in front of him, it was hard to remember what Rafik had wanted to tell him.

The boy studied the photographs on the wall, asked who this was and that. Was that Imelda with Rafik, was that Mubarak, was that Idi Amin, was that Mandela. He studied the shelves, running his fingers along the spines of the books, then the cartoons that had been framed and put up on the shelves. He selected one and brought it across to the desk, tilted it under the lamp's beam. It had faded only a little. In it, a caricature of Rafik swiped a sabre across a row of men's heads, dramatically large droplets of blood spattering onto him.

'What does it say?' Rafik said.

The boy read out the caption: '"All in a day's work."'

Rafik tapped it. 'They were always after me. That I was too this, too that, too tough, too close to the army. A man is many things. Sometimes he doesn't even know what.'

The boy replaced the frame on the shelf. He turned, parted the slats of the blinds with his fingers, and stared out onto the driveway. He nodded as though to himself.

'And you,' he said, 'are you alright?'

'Am I?' Rafik said. 'Yes, yes. A-one, first-class.'

The boy wanted to move the files stacked on and around the sofa to sit.

'Aaah, very good, very good,' Rafik said. 'This is why.' He remembered what he wanted to talk about. 'Other people ask me, I say, "No, it can only be the one person." You understand? To tell the story. I want you to.'

'What story?' The boy perched between the files.

'This one—' Rafik gestured at himself. 'Everyone tells the story they like. That I drink, that I hate women, that I'm too religious, that I'm a double-crosser, that I'm a chamcha. That I made this mistake, that I made that. That this is my fault, that that is. I want you to set the record straight.'

'Well—' The boy shifted about. 'How can I know your story? I can tell mine, the story of your'—he seemed to search for the word—'your'—as though it weren't obvious—'son. Not even that,' he said. 'You were so busy.'

'We will tell the facts,' Rafik said. He had a penknife in his hand and struck the desk with the hilt for emphasis. 'Look.' He nodded at the files. 'Open one, yes, see what it says.'

The boy reached for one of the files, brushed a little dust away. He had the delicate gestures of his mother, the same slender neck.

'Look inside,' Rafik said.

The boy glanced through it.

'Every record,' Rafik said. 'Every meeting, every letter. Anyone who says, "What kind of man was he?" The answer is here.' Rafik pointed at the file. 'Isn't it?'

'I suppose,' the boy said, patting the file shut. 'It's an archive.'

'Exactly,' Rafik said. 'And the value cannot be measured. Some—they want an airport with their name, a street, a college. I'm a humble man. But the facts, these are important to me.' The boy should start as soon as possible, Rafik said. There was a lot to go through and once he'd gone through it, he might have questions and then of course he would put it all on paper. 'Paper, this is what I wanted to say to you. It's what you do as well.'

The boy worried his heel against the ground. He opened his mouth and shut it, opened it again and, his eyes flickering towards the bookshelf, shut it. Finally, frowning at his lap, knotting his fingers together, he said, 'So, things are difficult.'

'You *do* need money,' Rafik said.

'I?' The boy looked up. 'No, I mean here, things are difficult here.'

'Here?'

'The house'—he gestured to the ceiling—'Mummy, the servants.'

'Always causing a fuss,' Rafik said. 'You don't listen to them.'

'It isn't a matter of listening or not,' the boy said, standing abruptly. 'I can see for myself. The cupboards are empty, the shelves are bare. And Mummy'—he cuffed his wrist—'all her jewellery gone, and her clothes, worn at the elbows, at the collar.'

'It's a show—'

'Paint peeling from the walls,' the boy went on, 'a crack along the front of the house, along the eaves, thick as my arm. The roof will collapse on your heads.' The boy turned to face the window. 'If the house is still yours. I've seen the papers. This notice from the court.'

'They say what they want,' Rafik said. 'These judges can be bribed like anyone else here.'

'But what difference does it make?' The boy spun around. 'It says they can take the house if you don't repay the loan. Why did you take these loans?'

'You've been away many years, you don't understand,' Rafik said. 'Sometimes you have a lot, sometimes you need a lot. If I can't buy fertiliser, then? If I can't buy cotton, then?'

He didn't need cotton anymore, did he? the boy said. The mill was gone. Long gone.

'Very sad,' Rafik said. 'All of them crooks.'

Didn't he see, the boy said, standing over the desk now so that his shadow fell across Rafik, that it was urgent, that things were terrible?

'Enough, enough—' Rafik stood too, pushing the lamp out of his face. 'Enough drama. You're too much like your mother. So, there are—' He couldn't find the word he meant. 'So? You and your mother want smooth sailing all your lives, nothing to worry you? I'm telling you, it's not like that. This is why you need toughness. I always said this to your mother. "He needs a backbone."'

'You're going in circles—' The boy's voice became high-pitched. 'You're not seeing. You'll lose this house. You'll have nowhere to live. Do you understand?'

'Who will take this house from me?' Rafik said. 'Who will dare? You show me the man. You bring him to me.' Something crashed from the table onto the floor, a pot of pens, the letter opener. 'No one will take this house. They can send a hundred letters. You give me the letter and I will tear it in front of your face.'

The room seemed suddenly too small for the two of them, the walls caving in.

'Everyone thinks they know best,' Rafik said. 'Even the servants telling you how to run your business.'

The boy chewed his lip and stared sullenly at the carpet. 'I came because I was asked,' he said.

Rafik hooked his arm around the boy's neck. He walked him out to the driveway. The files were brought out and stacked by the office to be loaded into the car for their journey the next day.

It was dusk now. The birds had become noisy. The sky was dark with them and it was as if the ground shook with their sounds: crows calling, buzzards and vultures shrieking as their shadows flickered across the concrete tiles.

FIFTEEN

IT WAS REMARKABLY ORDINARY. At first, he'd felt exhilarated by his return, then terrorized, there had been moments when his legs had wobbled, when seeing and remembering were like blows to his chest, but how quickly the strangeness, like the bright colour, like the noise, how quickly it had all faded.

How tiny his parents were, the size of children really, their clothes hanging off them like hand-me-downs, a brittleness to them, as though a gust from the overhead fan would shatter them. His mother was drab without her bangles and her chandelier earrings, without those rings on every finger, stones the size of quails' eggs. Her eyebrows were painted on. Lighting the oven, one day, she'd said, a flame had sparked, singeing them away. 'It isn't so bad,' she said. 'I can draw them how I want.'

His father's shirt was stained, it was torn at the collar. The servants were more presentable—Ayah was as she'd been the last time he'd seen her, decades ago. And yet, how quickly his

shock had dissipated, how quickly the details became fod-
der for notes, for scenes he sketched out in a pad for later,
reminding him of a funeral scene he'd written for a man not
unlike his father, a scene he'd never used, but searched for
now on his laptop unsuccessfully.

As diminished as his father was physically, he seemed
otherwise not so different at all. It was almost disappoint-
ing. He was as fierce, as relentless, as stubborn as he'd always
been. 'The house is falling down,' Fahad had said. 'There are
cracks in the roof, it will fall on your heads unless you do
something.'

'What cracks?' his father had said. 'All women's talk. All
mischief these servants and your mother are poisoning you
with.'

'And what about this letter?' Fahad had said. 'These loans,
that they'll take your house from you.'

'Let them,' he'd roared, shattering a paperweight against
the wall, sweeping his desk clear, as though those objects, the
lamp, the penknife, the inkwell, were somehow at fault.

'He's compos mentis,' Fahad had said to his mother. 'He'll
never let me sell Abad. It's pointless to try.'

'He's like this now, tomorrow he'll be gone, the next day
he'll be fine,' his mother had said, those odd eyebrows in-
expressive. 'You choose your moment. You sign the paper
yourself if you have to. There, anything goes. And for money
they'll do what you want, these officials.'

'I'll do what I can,' he'd said, saying the same to the
servants, who'd clustered around him in the yard between
their quarters, some of them crying, some of them gripping
on to him.

'I told you he would come,' Ayah had said to the others. 'I told you he would make it better, make it alright,' and Fahad had quickly ducked away.

IT HAD RAINED through the night, the rain drumming against the walls, an open window somewhere banging, so that Fahad had slept fitfully, dreaming himself at home in London, dreaming himself a boy again, dreaming himself on a train trundling upcountry.

In the morning it was raining still, thick sheets of rain flapping and swishing across the panes.

'You brought the weather with you,' his mother said. She'd sighed, 'Oh London,' and her gaze had flickered away somewhere past the top of his shoulder.

It continued to rain while they loaded the car, which was visible only in glimpses, the edge of a bonnet, the corner of a headlamp, light silvering a wing mirror like the moon was out.

His father supervised the loading of his files into the car and the old driver, who salaamed as he passed under the porch and then paused to clasp Fahad's hand with his wet fingers, was made to carry them one at a time back and forth, back and forth from the office beside the garage to where the car was parked, for some reason on the far side of the driveway.

The servants and his mother had come to the front door to see them off: the bearer solemnly holding a Koran over the threshold for them to pass beneath so that they should go with God's grace; Ayah touching her tiny hand to his shoulder, murmuring something he could not hear; his mother, when he glanced momentarily back, standing on the uppermost step,

the top half of her face obscured by the eaves, her jaw square
as a box.

WHEN THEY REACHED the toll booth that marked the city
limits the rain stopped. Now the car was steamy with damp
and a sweet, yeasty smell rose up from the upholstery.

Outside, there was desert and yellow sky and miles of
endless highway. No one spoke. Fahad watched for the mile-
stones along the side that counted down the distance to the
next town and listened to the thrum of the tyres on the tar-
mac. They passed a slow traffic of trucks on the left, their
cargos tarped and bulging, one stacked twice as high as the
truck itself, another twice as wide. The occasional rickshaw
or cart trundled along. And to the right, vans, buses, SUVs,
and hatchbacks sped past in a cloud of dust.

Fahad took notes, sketching out descriptions of the scen-
ery and the people in his notebook, his pencil jolting as the
tyres bumped in and out of potholes. The dunes were creased
with shadow and pocked with bramble. The horizon shimmered with heat. An old man was bent double at the helm
of a cart, the wind parting his beard like legs to either side of
his face, women were bundled into the back of a rickshaw
like sacks.

What had he been so afraid of? That coming back would
precipitate some sort of crisis? That it would surface memories that unmade him? That it would return him to some
earlier state—of doubt, of weakness, of wanting to disappear? It was nothing at all, it was only a place, only people,
and earth and sky, roads and cars, and walls, men and women
and children.

Fahad remembered a student he'd had a fondness for—
nothing irregular, only a fondness, something that drew him
to the boy, that made him seek him out in a workshop, made
him pay particular attention to what he said, to what he
wrote, the violence that shimmered beneath his prose.

Once they had sheltered from the rain under a doorway,
a side entrance on Gower Street to a college building, so narrow that Fahad's knuckles at one point knocked against the
boy's, a bead of rain creeping from the boy's temple down
his cheek and then curving along his jawbone, another drop
swelling in the notch above his lips, which Fahad imagined
brushing away with the tip of his thumb. It wasn't impropri-
ety that had stopped him from doing anything, it wasn't fear
of losing his job, it wasn't Alex: he'd thought of none of that.
He'd felt thrillingly like a boy again, more like a boy than he
felt here now.

The files in the trunk slid from side to side, front to back,
as the car changed lanes. The driver sped up and slowed down
and the files knocked around like a body. This business was
strangest of all, his father becoming almost agitated when he
spoke of the files. 'Everything is here,' he kept saying. 'Every
answer. What they say about me, the answer is here. All I did.'

Fahad wasn't uncurious about what might be in them—
it seemed to him, if he allowed himself to think of it, that
he was gathering material as if for a book: the notes he was
making, the scenes he was sketching.

His father in the front was still and craggy as a rock face.
He didn't seem to register the landscape or the traffic, except
for when the sunlight glared through the windscreen and he
lowered his visor.

That cartoon was right, of course: his father would chop

off as many heads as he needed to get where he wanted to,
even his cousin's, his son's. That was the irony. He'd done this
to himself. And now Abad was to be sold from under him.
Did he not understand? Could he just not show it? As if you
could understand, he thought, when you are never to blame
for anything.

There was no landscape—only desert. The river was out
of sight and no villages were to be seen. The horizon shimmered with what might be mountains.

Fahad talked about himself—how well he'd done, really,
the longlists he'd made, the shortlists, the fellowships, the
teaching job he'd been offered in Dubai, 'for good money,
unreasonably good money,' that he'd turned down because
he was too busy.

'Good, good,' his father said. He was the chancellor of
a university in Karachi, he said; he tried remembering its
acronym, tested out several names. 'Your mother will know,'
he said. 'They'll be happy for you to teach there, I'm sure,
if I tell them.' And this book, he continued, nodding again
towards the trunk, would get him many readers. 'It's not a
book about a man,' he said, 'but a country.'

THE TOWN BEGAN suddenly. Suddenly, carts, rickshaws, and
trucks piled up ahead. Those on foot darted between them.
Shops encroached from either side so that the road narrowed
and the car had to slow to a crawl. People became a procession and the car followed as it turned to the left, past a bar-
ricade, where a guard, lazing in a chair to one side, indicated
they should turn around. He did not, it seemed, recognise
Fahad's father.

When the driver gave his father's name to the man, the man frowned, tilted his head to one side. Fahad's father struggled angrily to open the car door. Unable to for some reason, he leaned across the driver and bellowed at the man, raised his hand as though he'd strike him if he were within reach and then the man hurried up, salaaming, begging forgiveness, unlooped the rope that tied the boom to a post, so that it swung up and they passed beneath it.

The path led between a high wall and stalls selling rose petals, tinsel garlands, nuts, and sweets. At a gate in the wall, they were questioned again, this guard glancing back in the direction they'd come, peering into the car and giving a signal, at which point the gate opened. They drove onto a marble concourse, with arches all around it. Under one arch there was a ceremonial wooden door and beyond it a golden dome glittering in the sun.

He'd wait here, Fahad said, but his father insisted that he come.

'You must,' he said. 'It is a must. This saint is our most revered—' He pointed in the direction of the dome, and then climbed out of the car. If he said anything else, Fahad didn't hear it.

Guards clustered around his father, bowing, clasping his hand. Fahad and his father left their shoes beside a doorway. The marble tiles were worn shallow at its threshold, the doorway worn at the edges too, perhaps by a drifting tide of hands. They were guided into a cool shadowy chamber, through another doorway, through another chamber, to a steep staircase leading down to the shrine, its dome rising above them, filling the sky.

The steps were strewn with figures: a legless urchin, a mother and child, a shirtless fakir, his white beard beaded, his hair twisted into thick dreads. Fahad offered his father his arm but his father charged forward alone, even speeding up a little, tripping down the steps two, three at a time.

Inside, the shrine was twice as high as it was broad, the ceiling tiled with mirrorwork that shattered the room into a constellation.

His father was accosted by a beggar who seemed to know him, who spoke animatedly in his own language, whom his father greeted by name, putting his arm around the man's bare shoulders.

People were singing in various corners, the light slanting through high windows so that a figure here, a figure there was illuminated: an old woman with a tika, a swaying child, a square-headed giant.

A wooden structure stood in the centre of the room. The worshippers crowding round it were pushed aside so that he and his father could enter. Inside, there was a cage and inside that lay a mound in the shape of a person, draped with brightly coloured cloths, a garlanded totem at its head.

How would he describe this and how would he describe that, Fahad wondered. How would he describe the voices coming from all around, from above and below, the heady fragrance of rose petals that tickled the back of his throat, the air thrumming with attention, how would he describe every soul, every spirit directed towards the same object of devotion.

They were given cloths to arrange upon the mound, encouraged to touch it, to pray. His father's lips moved in prayer and the men who were with them, they prayed too but with their eyes flickering towards the peripheries of the room, distant thoughts passing across their faces like shadows.

He directed his mind again and again to the details—to the bare bulbs inside the tomb, to the gold and copper threads woven into the shrouds that sparked like the edges of blades, to the voices wailing in lament—but the music, the bright light that came from both outside and inside the cage, made every detail somehow more than itself so that his father's arm silvered with hair, his sleeve pushed up to the elbow by the bars that he reached between, his hand worn as an old glove, there was something in that gesture that was, like the song, entirely free of time and place. Fahad wanted to clasp that hand, he wanted to interlace his fingers with those fingers, and looking at his own, tilting his own under the light, it was the same hand, it was the same, it was the same. His father was pale as a ghost, pale as the moon behind a cloud. He disappeared into his clothes, as though his clothes were a veil. Fahad imagined taking his hand, imagined diving between these bars into this cage, imagined the bars turning to dust, the walls turning to light, so that there was only sky and sky and sky, dark and endless as night, and he, he expanded beyond himself, he was his father too and now they were the sky, they shimmered with a thousand stars, so that the music was their bodies, the clamour of voices, and the people were them, and he was lying in this tomb and he was looking upon it and he was touching it and he was being touched and the song they were singing became words, and the words became, 'Ali, Ali, Ali, Ali, Ali.'

IT WAS LIKE he had stumbled through a door and on the other side was only the past, so that as they emerged from the shrine out into the sunlight in the forecourt, as his father handed wads of thousand-rupee notes to the officials outside, as they nosed their way through the crowded streets out of the town, as they emerged onto the highway, the mountains suddenly upon them, casting a deep shadow across the road, he was a boy in Abad again, hiding behind a book on his bed on the landing, he was whirling giddily through a gathering, lights flashing like warnings, he was rattling over the bumps and divots in the dirt tracks across the farm, he was kicking off his sandals, pushing aside ferns and branches, stepping through the soft earthen floor of the copse, something scuttling through the undergrowth, the boy Ali catching his arm.

His father became voluble, talking now about the shrine, how the road to it had been built by a man whose prayers to have a child were finally answered there, talking about an ancient fortress hidden in these mountains, talking about the first Edh sacrifice he could remember, the bullock juddering, shitting in thick ropes as blood spurted from a gash cut into its neck, how surprisingly difficult the beast had been to kill.

Now it seemed they were hurtling unstoppably towards Abad, their tyres reeling up miles of road. Fahad braced his back against his seat, an arm against the door, his heels against the mat in the seat well, twisting his head out of the sunlight through the window. The dampness in the copse, the sweet smell of the mulch, the dew that glittered at the points of leaves like the whites of eyes in the dark, a breeze tickling the hairs on the back of his neck, the ice cream sundaes at that hotel swirled with bright colour, crimson and purple and yellow, studded with shards of ice sharp as glass, and the

inevitability of Ali, who was the logic that ordered everything before him and the only possible outcome.

They came upon a town and his heart beat harder. They
idled at a railway crossing waiting for a train to pass and then
swung across it into the busy heart of the place, Fahad searching wildly for familiar sights and finding none in the mud-
dle of people and rickshaws and ramshackle buildings, the
children playing games, the vendors selling fruit, vegetables,
chaat, the noise here of the town mingling with the noise of
the jungle—each sound shouting a warning or a threat. The
air became dim with smoke and the figures disappeared into
it. The car turned and turned and now they went through a
gate and stopped by a tree, lines of chalk radiating outwards
from a doorway beneath the tree.

Why were they stopping? Fahad wondered. Were they
breaking their journey at somebody's home? Fahad's heart
slowed at the prospect of delay. As a small cluster of servants
greeted his father, the luggage was unloaded, the car bouncing
each time a case was removed. He scanned the faces outside.
He had been looking, he realised, for Ali since the moment
he had reached Pakistan, since the moment his mother had
called, since before that even, looking for his features amongst
passers-by on the street over the years, amongst passengers
at Heathrow as he'd boarded his flight here, amongst those
milling about the airport when he'd reached Karachi, with
increasing frenzy amongst the others on the road on this journey, amongst the pilgrims at the shrine, amongst those in this
town whatever it was, looking for his dark eyes, his mouth,
which twisted at the corners. Of course, the Ali he was looking for was long gone, was someone entirely different now,
Fahad knew that, but still he kept looking.

He climbed out of the car, and several of the servants greeted him, guided him up the shallow porch steps into a verandah, past a lawn burnt yellow, past trees cut down to their stumps, to another door into a hallway, where a life-size photograph of his father stood facing him.

IT WAS ABAD. It was the house. The hallway became a version of the hallway he remembered, the walls leaning precariously in on either side, brass wall lamps burnt at the sconces. He stopped.

'It's Abad,' he said to the servant carrying his bag, who stopped now too.

'Sir?' the man said.

But it couldn't be. Here, the town came up to the walls of the house, as though the house were under siege. He hurried out again. It was almost too dark to see. There had been an avenue of trees before, and the town, the chimneys of the mills, in the far distance. Now even the noise of the place beat against the walls, beat into the space between the walls, so that it seemed as though every part of the house trembled with the shrieking traffic, the horns, the engines, voices calling, a dog howling, a dog barking.

Inside, was it as he remembered? He couldn't be sure anymore whether this wall had been here, that picture, this room. Upstairs, yes, the landing was untouched, as still as a diorama. The narrow daybed was there against the wall, the bookshelf opposite, with his copy of *The Far Pavilions* and *Macbeth*, which he thumbed through to find notes he'd scribbled into the margins in pen. But the servant had continued on through a door on the far wall. They'd entered a room identical in its layout to his father's room, as he remembered it, the bed and a sitting area arranged identically, a dressing room, a bathroom beyond it.

'This is new,' he said, finding himself somewhat breathless.

'Sir?' the man said again. He had set Fahad's case onto the coffee table, and stood to attention before it, in a grimy kurta, unshaven, his hair slick with grease.

'The room,' Fahad said.

'It's not right?' the man said. He rounded the table to switch on the air conditioner, which droned, then spluttered clouds of ash, then switched itself off, then came back on again. 'It's very old,' the man said.

A small, high grilled window looked out onto the lawn. In the fading light, the tree stumps looked like men who had scaled the boundary wall.

'The guest room downstairs is not right,' the man said. 'Otherwise there's your father's room. It has two beds.'

'It wasn't here before,' Fahad said, pointing at the floor. The man dipped his head as though he were nodding.

There had been an entrance on this wall to the terrace, yes. He returned to the landing and found it. But not a door to another room. He opened that door again, glanced in, where the man still stood, hands clasped, head bowed.

The door to the terrace was bolted and he had to wobble the bolt loose. The door clattered open, banging against the wall. For a moment the setting sun shone directly in his face and in the glare he saw the fields, golden all the way to the horizon, smoke spiralling from a village fire, a herd of buffalo snaking across a track, and like jewels, women and children in their bright clothes studded amongst the swaying grass. Then the sun dipped below the ledge of the terrace and he could see clearly and there were no fields at all.

The space was barely the size of the landing and had a high wall around it that obscured the view till he was right at the edge, standing up on a raised platform of bricks that ran along the perimeter. Here was the town, its lean-tos and half-built homes piling up so close they might topple in. He followed the ledge around the side of the house.

The sun was low, the shadows long, so that nothing seemed separate from anything else. The ramshackle houses continued in a ragged row from the boundary wall, alongside a broad swathe of savannah, bramble, and feathery wild grasses, gold and green and copper, that swayed now, that bowed, that flattened like a mane.

SIXTEEN

THE BOY WAS IN strange spirits, driving the jeep erratically, too slow, too fast, the gears too low, too high, swerving round corners, bumping through ditches, Rafik having at times to tug the wheel straight. The car stalled and then the boy couldn't restart it, pulling the choke too long.

'You've flooded it,' Rafik said.

'Because it stopped,' the boy said, knocking his fists against the wheel. 'And this doesn't work.' He turned the knob of the air conditioner and it blasted them with hot air.

'If you'll be here, you replace it,' Rafik said. 'Get a new one.'

The boy climbed out to let the driver restart the car.

'You let him do it,' Rafik said, but once the car had started, the boy insisted the driver return to the back again.

'There are no roads,' the boy said.

'The roads are there,' Rafik indicated, 'you just look.' He wound his window up and the branches of the trees along the track scraped the glass and the chassis.

'It was the one thing you said,' the boy said. '"There should always be a way around." You said'—the boy glanced at the men at the back in the rearview mirror—'"They don't want you to see, so they allow the roads to flood, to grow over." You said that. The first job you did, when your father gave you the land, after you levelled it, was to make roads, so you could see every field for yourself.'

'Very good,' Rafik said, signalling to the boy that where the track diverged he should take the path to the left. 'Who are you looking for? There's no one.' The boy was searching wildly, left and right. 'You're being nervous.'

'I can't see,' he said. 'It's all overgrown.'

'We learnt to hunt here, my brother and I,' Rafik said. 'There were wild boar in those days. We were so little the guns were too heavy to carry alone. They would hold them from the back for us to shoot. An ugly sport. Like these men who take their guards with them where they go. Is the power in the man or his guns?'

Rafik directed him up the slope.

'Well I'm glad you have a guard now,' the boy said. 'You should keep him with you.'

'These people, the police and so on, have insisted. There were troubles in the elections, the other side firing at me, tearing the shirt off my back. They said, "You must keep a gunman." I said, "Leave it. It's not for a man like me."' Rafik shrugged.

The track ascended and they emerged from tall grasses onto the canal bank. The boy slowed the car, glancing through the window into the canal. Finally, he stopped. He climbed out. 'He takes an interest,' Rafik said to the men.

'Now he'll sort you all out. He's telling me, "What are they doing? They're doing nothing. You should throw them out, all of them."'

The boy peered over the edge of the bank. 'Look,' he said, 'at the plastic bags and cigarette cartons.'

'They empty their sewers into the canal,' one of the men said. 'They empty their rubbish. Before they wouldn't dare.'

'You wouldn't have allowed it before,' the boy said. 'And these men doing nothing, making a wilderness of the farm, you'd have beaten them with the back of your hand, you'd have thrown them in jail.'

And why was it dry, the boy wanted to know.

The men explained that water came in the summer, not the winter, that theirs was a rice-growing region.

Yes, he knew all that, the boy said. So had there been water in the summer?

There had not, they said, shuffling their feet, frowning at the ground.

'They're good-for-nothings,' Rafik said, 'know-nothing, do-nothing, good-for-nothing.'

A motorcycle swerved past them, then a small truck. 'It was jungle when my father gave it,' Rafik said.

The boy wanted to know who it was, crossing their land.

It was a bypass now, one of the men explained, to get to the other side of the city.

The boy shielded his eyes from the glare, looked out across the fields. 'They're so close now,' he said. 'All these houses. The town has swallowed up the farm. The houses will be here sooner or later.' He gestured around him. 'They're waiting.' He pointed at the shacks in the distance.

'Let them—' Rafik shook his head. 'Let them wait till I'm dead.'

They climbed back into the car, the boy jogging his knee, worrying the heel of his hand against the wheel.

'Things change,' the boy said. 'You can't hold on forever. You're not even here most of the time.'

'Don't do this,' Rafik said, touching the boy's hand to steady it.

'Now the villages are made of brick,' the boy said, slowing as he rounded a corner. 'The walls and dwellings. The mud came from the land and would return to the land. But these brick homes. They're going nowhere.'

He idled by a gate in the wall. 'There'd always be children,' he said. 'You'd have toffees for them.'

Rafik sent his manager to see where the children were.

The boy pointed unhappily at the cars parked beside the gate.

The village men worked in the town, the driver said from the back of the car. There wasn't enough money in farming. They'd all found jobs: mechanics, shopkeepers, all sorts.

The manager returned, shepherding a small group of children, and instructed them to hold their hands out. The driver scrabbled round in the back of the car, reached between the seats, hunted in and under the dashboard. There were no toffees in the car after all.

'We had a friend from this village,' Rafik said. He asked after the man. Was he still alive?

That man had left some years ago, they said, shifted his family to Karachi, where his son was a nurse.

'Now they send their children to school and cover their

women,' Rafik said. 'He's going to fix you all,' Rafik told the men again, nodding towards Fahad, 'and all this lot'—he gestured back at the village—'now that he's come.'

What about his father's other friends in Abad, the boy wanted to know. He remembered others, coming to the house, other landowners.

'You see where we are now?' Rafik said, tapping the dashboard. 'You always used to ask. This is where this woman is buried, this saint, they call her. You see the path. They allow everything to grow wild, but this, no, this they keep tidy as a lawn.'

Stones pinged against the undercarriage. 'You're going off the road,' Rafik told him, straightening the wheel.

'I can't see—' The boy swerved this way and that.

'Don't become nervous,' Rafik said.

The boy bumped over rocks and hillocks.

'If you don't know where you're going, then stop,' Rafik said. 'The driver is better.'

But it seemed as though the boy was unable to stop, careering past a tree, past a boulder.

'Stop, if you don't know,' Rafik said, taking the wheel again to hold it steady, and now the boy braked so suddenly that the men at the back were flung against the front seats, knocking Rafik against the dashboard, the boy against the wheel, something striking the windscreen. The engine spluttered and then failed.

'If you can't see,' Rafik said, shoving himself into his seat, a pain corkscrewing through his knee as he pushed with his heel, 'you should go slow.'

The boy seemed dazed. He looked about. In the windscreen, directly in front of his face, the glass had splintered like a bull's-eye.

The men at the back rearranged themselves, their weight wobbling the vehicle.

'Are you alright?' Rafik said.

'I thought I saw something,' the boy said—a tremor in his voice, his hands gripping the wheel—'something move.'

'You have a—' Rafik tapped his own cheek to show there were grazes on the boy's.

'My glasses,' the boy said, and bent over, groping between the seats, emerging with a handful of broken pieces: a lens, a toffee wrapper, some bits of plastic. 'I don't know—' he began, the pieces falling between his fingers onto his lap.

'You let the driver—' Rafik said, patting him on the shoulder, but the boy remained where he was, picking up pieces from his lap, holding up a splinter sharp as a needle. 'You let him,' Rafik said, looking down the hood of the vehicle, to see if there was any impact from a collision.

'I saw someone,' the boy said again. 'Or an animal.'

'Come,' Rafik said. 'You let the driver.'

The door stuck and then, once the boy could open it, it caught in a bush of thorny branches, so that the driver, pulling his sleeve over his hand, had to beat them, kick them away.

VISITORS HAD COME to see Rafik. The power was off and so they sat outside on the verandah, one of the servants fanning him with a folded newspaper. They asked about his health, asked about the state of the country, would the army come in again, would there be elections, would he contest, would the boy, was that why he'd returned?

'He can understand,' Rafik said, nodding at the boy. 'He can say for himself.'

The boy looked blindly at the lawn. He rubbed his eyes with his knuckles and blinked.

'They're asking,' Rafik said, 'if it will be you now. Over here.'

No, no, the boy said.

'It's an old family,' one of the visitors said, 'the oldest name. When people say Abad, it is your name they are saying. How can a name like that disappear? It cannot. Never.'

He was barely sixteen when his father had passed and he'd inherited the lands, Rafik said. 'A man cannot stay a child when he has things to care for.'

Was the boy married, the visitor wanted to know, and when he discovered the boy was unmarried, said, 'But he's old enough. He should have married years ago. You ask your father to find you someone,' he told the boy. 'The daughter of this one—' He named a notable family. 'Or that—' He named another.

The boy frowned. 'Should I tell you what to do?' he said to the visitor.

'We say it from love,' the visitor said. 'A family like this, it belongs to all of us, it is our family.'

'World leaders,' another visitor said to the boy, 'have come to Abad because of your father. History has happened here in Abad because of your father.'

'History,' Rafik said, remembering at once the files he'd brought with him. He sent for them, had them stacked in front of him so that he could explain to the visitors what they were. 'No one has kept records like this,' Rafik said. 'Every date, every letter, every meeting, it's all in here.' He tapped the uppermost file. 'And he is going to make a book from this.'

The visitors agreed that there should be a book, that so many other lesser people had books about them, that this should be in schools, that it was important.

'It is,' Rafik said. 'Not for me. But for—' And he spread an arm out to include everyone really. The files should be taken to the office he'd made, he told a servant. 'I made it for this,' Rafik said to the boy. 'You see. Go, go.'

The boy argued that without his glasses he was lost, that one room looked just like another.

They were having his glasses repaired at the market, Rafik told the boy. 'Don't make such a fuss. I had this office made for you.'

Someone would have to guide him there, the boy said finally, and Rafik called a servant to take his arm.

SEVENTEEN

FAHAD COULD SEE objects within several inches of his face but anything further away was blurred. Without his glasses it was as though he were submerged underwater, life happening above the surface, sounds reaching him more slowly.

He kept seeing Ali wherever he turned. Was that him under an arch of the verandah? Was that him appearing from inside the house, the screen door slamming shut behind him? Was that him striding down the yard, as a servant guided Fahad across it, the man's hand light as a bird on Fahad's arm? If it's him, Fahad told himself, if it's him, I'll, I'll, I'll, and he made all sorts of promises in his head.

It was in fact the gatekeeper, bringing keys that he tried in the lock of a door under an awning: one, then another, then another, then another till he found one that fit and shoved the door open.

The servant who had accompanied him fiddled with the light switches inside. The bulbs might need changing, he said, when none came on.

'I can't see anyway,' Fahad said, but the man shone the screen of his phone to light the room.

All wood, the man said, the walls and the ceiling and the floor. It had come at great cost from Quetta and the lamp fittings were brass, and this desk came from one of his father's government offices.

It was entirely abstract to Fahad. Shards of sun cut through the gloom here and there, and the air had the smell and feel of sawdust.

No one had used it since it was built, the servant said, and he was a young man then, helping in the kitchen on no salary at all. 'But you didn't come,' the man said, 'and all these years it's been like this.' He gestured at the empty room.

His father's files were brought in and piled up on the desk. One servant instructed another to dust the room, to sweep the floor, to change the lights and fix the blinds.

They shouldn't do all this on his account, Fahad said. He wouldn't stay long.

But outside, he paused a moment in the centre of the yard. A hot wind buffeted him, pushing him forward, swelling his shirt like a parachute. He had a sudden vision of himself out in the jeep crossing the lands, as though he were there day after day, under an enormous sky, the heat crackling through the tall, burnished grain and the dry leaves, a shimmering wisp on the track slowly revealing an approaching figure.

HE SAT AWHILE on the landing, hugged his knees to his chest, and felt like a boy again, with that same stomach-wobbling feeling of urgency, which made him get up and walk the peri-meter of the space, trailing his fingers against the banister of the staircase and the wall, bumping into an armchair, into a coffee table. The feeling, a feeling that he must do something, he must act, but what, but what, but what?

HIS FATHER WAS a little frail, it was true, frailer than he should have been at his age, whatever that was now, and sometimes he was a little confused. They'd only been in Abad a night and he'd told Fahad to take him home.

'Home? Where do you mean? You *are* home,' Fahad had said. 'Do you want to go to Karachi?'

'No, no,' he'd said. And then repeated, with emphasis, 'Home.'

Fahad had asked the servants and they'd answered, some of them more hesitantly than others, that Sahib was quite alright, that he was fine, that he'd come to Abad after a year or more, not since the elections, that to lose the second election, that was harder for him than the first, after that his hair had turned white.

TO BE ALONE was better, and here, here he felt more alone than he'd ever been, though there were people everywhere, with their needs, their wants, their hunger, their fear. He understood religion. He understood a man falling upon his knees, clasping his hands above his head and asking the heavens to act for him. He listened for footsteps up the staircase, watched for shadows on the wall, stood finally at the banister, peering down into the stairwell.

———

FAHAD WAS STANDING on the terrace, looking out over the wilderness that the farm had become, the sun fading from the sky, the fields a stormy sea streaked with surf, when he heard sirens. A stream of black sluicing down the street towards their house could be, he thought, a convoy of vehicles, pouring in through the gate—flashing lights suggesting that some were police vans, some perhaps SUVs with blacked-out windows, and were these trucks of guards, who now, as the vehicles piled into the yard, clambered out, stamping their boots in the dirt like a drumroll.

From the landing he heard loud voices and footsteps, and then a servant materialised halfway up the staircase to announce that he had visitors.

He asked who they were but didn't listen for the name. These people were asking after Fahad, the servant said. His father was sleeping. Should he send them away? 'They think they are important,' the servant said, as Fahad followed him down. 'He would beg at your father's feet, now he has to show what a big man he is,' the servant said. 'Not even a hundred acres he had before. Now he has thousands. But everyone knows it was money and guns that got him his position. Otherwise who would have voted for him?'

AT THE BOTTOM of the staircase, Fahad felt suddenly so disoriented he didn't know for a moment which way to turn. The stairwell was dark and he could barely see the servant in his shabby kurta. He asked why the lights weren't on. They were switched on for him then and he saw, remembering at the same time, that the corridor turned to the left. At the end of the hallway, beyond the drawing room, there was a waiting area and it was crowded with murmuring figures, but in the drawing room there was only one, who, after a moment, stood to greet Fahad. The way that he stood, the broadness of him, his voice that came at Fahad from all around, it knocked the breath out of Fahad's chest.

'Is it you?' Fahad said, his voice unnatural, almost a whisper. The terrifying magic of the place, it had brought him here, it had charted every step, and the past unspooled in front of him as though there were screens across his eyes: his years in London, his lovers, a glittering whirl of dinners and friends, of holidays and places he'd lived, Oxford, those terrible years, then his last summer in Abad, Ali, Ali, Ali, the farm and his father, Mousey, water surging through the canal, children skipping alongside the jeep, screaming outside a village gate, fields rippling with grain, stalks bowing under their weight, and the sky immense with possibility.

But as Ali, having stepped nearer, having spread his arms to embrace Fahad, leaned in, tilting his cheek to Fahad's, he became someone else entirely. It wasn't Ali at all. It wasn't. Fahad laughed.

'It isn't,' he said. 'I'm free. I'm free of it.'

'Brother,' the man said. 'It's been many years. When we met last we were both boys.'

Fahad didn't remember him at all, thinking instead that it should have been Ali, that he had to find him, that the past was like a poison that never left your body.

The man led Fahad to the sofa where he'd been sitting as though this were his house.

What respect he'd always had for this family, the man

said. He would come to this house as a boy, he wanted to learn from Sahib, he would see him on TV with the president, with generals, in other countries meeting their leaders, a man from Abad, what a thing. 'I said one day, God willing, it will be me.'

Tea was brought and the man gave a curt instruction to the bearer to deliver to some attendant of his outside. 'The troubles you've had,' he said, 'a giant like your father, a king of this country, of the world, how can I watch like the others if he suffers? I must act.' He drank his tea in the fashion of Fahad's father, pouring it from the cup into the saucer and tipping the saucer to his lips. No one else of course could afford to buy a farm like Rafik's unless it was sold a piece at a time, the man said. In the old days, when there was water, it was much more valuable but now any buyer would have to spend an exorbitant amount, digging tube wells or converting the land to some other use. He discussed various possible rates for the land, but it was no good to him, he said, without the house, no good at all, he wouldn't bother without the house, he had plenty of land, five thousand acres and a beautiful bungalow too but not as well situated as theirs. This would be useful for him.

In the midst of the conversation, the bearer reappeared with a tray, upon which sat a dish, and on the dish, a pair of glasses for Fahad, comically large, gaudy gold frames, but suddenly to see clearly again was startling.

How could he have mistaken this man for Ali? This man was squat, pot-bellied, with a cone-shaped head that narrowed at the crown and a prayer stain on the centre of his forehead.

'Sir—' The man stood suddenly, the tea spilling from his saucer, dribbling onto the hem of his kurta.

Fahad's father was in the open doorway, between the sheers that were ordinarily drawn across it. He was pale as a wraith, his white hair unruly, his eyes the colour of gunmetal.

The man bowed, approached his father bowing still, holding his hands out, introducing himself as Mustafa something. Fahad's father pushed his hands away.

'Why is this fellow here?' his father said. 'He's a waste of time.' Then he turned and disappeared down the hallway.

Mustafa studied the splatter of tea across his kurta, rang the servants' bell, and called for a cloth and some water. When it came, he wet the cloth and dabbed at the mark.

His slippers were brightly embroidered. On a swarthy wrist, he wore a gold Rolex with a black face and when he moved his hand the light made sharp points on the bezel of the watch.

He was only here another day, Fahad said. It probably wouldn't be possible to do all this in a day.

'In five minutes,' Mustafa said, holding up his fingers. 'The officials here, they are happy to please me.'

And his father, Fahad said, 'He has strong opinions. This is his home.'

It would always be his home, Mustafa said. A king like that, he didn't need a house, he didn't need land for his home to be here. 'All of Abad is his home,' he said. It was too late now, but he would return the following day with the registrar, with the papers. 'It's as easy as this,' he said, and scribbled in the air.

Fahad saw him out, the crowd in the hallway clustering behind them as they passed through it, out to the verandah, out to the yard, where an SUV with tinted windows was idling. There were others behind it, several police trucks, which

sounded their sirens again now and trucks of plainclothes se-
curity guards, Kalashnikovs slung round their shoulders.

Once they had left, the yard was empty but for a child
knocking a stick against a pillar, breaking it into increasingly
shorter lengths. Fahad turned back to the house to find his
father.

EIGHTEEN

RAFIK WOKE TO a terrible sound, which he listened for again, to be sure it belonged to the world and not to a dream. After a pause, it recurred—a howl, so terrible, of such suffering, suffering of limitless depth. And then again, breaking despairingly in its higher register.

He waited for it to stop. When it continued, he turned away from it, buried his head against his pillow, but he heard it still, calling, it seemed, for him, calling, in its own way, his name.

So he sat up. He swivelled round, set his feet on the ground. He stood. He approached the window. It gave out onto the verandah, which was unlit, as in fact the whole area was at this time of night. He saw nothing but a glimmer that could have been his moonlit reflection.

The sound was so mournful, and yet there was also a note in it of desperate, desperate hope that jittered through him. He lay down. But it came and it came and it came, straining a little now, calling for him a little more desperately.

The front door was bolted and in the dark he groped a while, feeling along the upper edge of the casement, till he found the bolt and loosened it. The sound became louder and more wretched, though the gaps between each call were sometimes so long, he worried, till the call came, that it might not come again.

It was the sound of pain, and he imagined a bloody wound, a leg caught in a rusting trap, a stomach swollen with disease. It became a human sound, then an animal sound, an animal sound, then a human sound. He imagined a mother's call, and that quickened his heart and his steps.

He followed it along the verandah to the far wall and then, as it grew more distant, back through the porch door, round to the garages on the left. There was a full moon and the yard was desolate. A fine grit underfoot gave him a kind of steadiness.

A small wooden gate led onto the lands. It was a gate for clandestine visits and he remembered the horse carriage that brought Soraya her lunch at school. He'd help her climb the wall to get it, interlocking his fingers to make a stirrup of his hands. He'd stand guard. He remembered the plaits she'd wear halfway down her back, that she'd toss away from him, that he'd tug when he could grab them. Once, she had held her head still, tipped it towards him so that the plaits hung in front of him like bell ropes, and he'd shrugged, he'd tapped them away.

Beyond the gate, the earth was harder with sharp-edged rocks in places and tall grasses that brushed against his arms and cheeks. A hot gust of wind scattered small stones against his ankles and brought with it a sweet, smoky smell like wheat chaff, like hard work.

The path climbed to the top of a hillock and the lands below him spread out like an ocean before a journey. When he heard the call again, now faint with fear, with frailty, as though it might not call again, he knew exactly where it came from.

NINETEEN

FAHAD BARELY SLEPT, turning and turning in his bed, the sheets damp with sweat, turning one way then the other, turning onto his back, then his side, then his stomach. What else could he do but sell the farm? How to repay the loans if not from the proceeds of the sale? Wasn't there anything else? And once it was sold, it was gone forever. It could never be unsold. But would anyone dare displace his father from any home of his? It couldn't happen.

Abad is just an idea, he told himself, whether the land is in your name or not. If you sell it, you can think of it still, as you have all these years. Return to it, even if only in your head, and it will be as much yours as anything has ever been. But have you really thought of it at all? It seemed to him that he had, he had, that he couldn't remember a moment when he hadn't thought of Abad, memories of the place shimmering through every memory since he'd left: the beaten brass of its fields, its sky silvered like a platter, its searing breeze. But to remember what wasn't his, to remember something

he didn't have and could never have again, it was a different remembering, it was remembering loss, loss that recurred
endlessly and now the thought prompted him to remember loss after loss: that last idyllic summer at Oxford, Mike,
a cobbled hillside in Crete, their sweet old brandy-coated
cocker Booze, Alex at the very start, the little girl they hadn't
adopted, everything he thought he'd be and have.

He thought again of Ali, of how startlingly Abad had become something else after he met him, how he and Ali had
raced along the country roads, around the town, and it had
belonged to them, every street corner, every patch of earth,
every fruit stall and mechanic and that old cinema showing blue movies, and the Christian cemetery with its broken
wall, with its spells tied up in plastic bags in the branches of
trees.

He paced up and down the room, then round and round
the landing, finally out on the terrace cornering the ledge like
a man in a cell. Why should anyone think twice if he asked
after Ali, and if they did, what did it matter? He'd be gone
in a day. He might never return—that last thought cutting
through him like a knife.

So when the bearer brought his breakfast, Fahad, after
talking about the power cuts, about the heat, complaining
that the water dribbled from the tap in his bathroom, asked
what had become of that friend of his father who had the
son, what was the son's name, his eyes flitting around his teacup like a fly, they'd come to the house, they had land here.

The bearer knotted his hands together in front of his lap.
Sahib was not in his room, he said. He was nowhere in the
house. He was not on the compound.

He'd be outside nearby somewhere, Fahad said. He did

this sometimes in Karachi. He went for walks at night if he couldn't sleep. And why shouldn't he? Perhaps his room had been warm, perhaps he'd ventured out in search of a breeze.

'Yes, sir,' the man said.

Fahad sent for his father's manager. The man appeared thumbing a rosary. 'God keep him safe,' he said.

'He's alright,' Fahad said. 'He'll be only here. How far can he have gone?'

The man nodded.

Did he remember this family, Fahad asked, describing Ali and his father.

'Yes,' the man said. 'An important family. The son sits on the municipal council. A good man. A tough man.'

Fahad felt giddy. His teacup wobbled so terribly he had to set it down.

'Admirers of your father,' the man continued. But then, he gave their names and it was somebody else.

He could remember the way, Fahad thought. He'd drive down to their farm to see for himself.

After he dressed, he glanced in his father's room to make sure his father wasn't there. The sheets were rumpled. The TV was on but the screen was black, emitting only a low hum. The dressing room and bathroom were empty too. He glanced into the drawing room and dining room to be certain. The yard was bustling with servants, with visitors Fahad didn't recognise.

The front gate was ordinarily locked at night, he was told, and the gatekeeper kept the key on a hook in his quarters but, for some reason that was not immediately clear, it had not been locked that night or morning.

So then, Fahad said, his father had wandered out into the

street, into the town perhaps. Perhaps the town was what his
father had meant by home.

The group followed him to the front gate and out onto
the dirty street that led past it. It was already busy with traffic, with beggars and carts and people going about their business. 'He'll be only here—' Fahad gestured down the street.

'God is our master,' one of them said, as though someone
had died.

FAHAD TOOK THE little jeep. He'd drive himself, he said. All
of you, he told the crowd, you look this way, you look that,
you look in the bazaar, in all these little alleys. It was to keep
them busy more than anything else. The old man couldn't
have gone far.

But as he drove the jeep out into the road, swerving
around a donkey cart that was crossing, he remembered the
strange things his father had said to the visitor the previous
evening.

FAHAD TOOK A wrong turn and had to double back. He
turned right when he should have turned left. The town had
swallowed up so much of the farmland around it, he wondered
whether Ali's farm still existed, whether these ramshackle
houses here, this mechanic, this chakki grinding wheat into
flour, *were* in fact the farm, but suddenly, beyond them, he
recognised a chipped milestone along the open road, beyond
it the dirt track they'd rattled down, and, narrowly avoiding a
speeding van, he swung onto it, his palms so slick with sweat,
his grip slipped along the wheel.

HE REMEMBERED WILDERNESS here, but now there were fields on either side, the earth ploughed into neat furrows. Overhead, though there was no sun, the sky was a bright, almost fluorescent, yellow. It seemed to him as if the car were driving itself, as if he could lift his hands off the wheel and his feet off the pedals and the car would continue on.

The road curved past a cluster of trees and, beyond it, in a clearing, framed by vegetation, was the old brick house. The car picked up speed, bouncing through ditches, knocking him side to side, up and down, the tyres spraying stones and dust.

He parked the car at the edge of the forecourt, leaving himself for some reason a great distance to cross on foot. He had learnt to shoot behind this house, Ali's arms around his, steadying him, firing into the beams of the headlamps, anticipating the shriek of glass shattering, so that sometimes he'd heard it even when it hadn't happened and he'd had to ask, 'Did I? Did I hit it?'

Only when he was a few feet away from the front door did he discover it wasn't there at all. Tall, feathery grasses bristled from the doorframe. The windows were smashed. Swinging around, he saw that there were no cars but his parked in the forecourt. There were no servants lazing in the shade of the trees.

He stepped through the doorway. The house was only a facade. The wall at the back had fallen away completely. The staircase hung from the half of the ceiling that remained, its lowest step still some feet off the ground. And the ground was rocks and stones, bushes and weeds. Was it the wrong

place? He surveyed it again from the forecourt outside, trying to reconstruct the house from his memory, its door with
iron studs and an iron hoop for a knocker. Weren't there
steps here? Was the roof tiled and pitched?

Movement inside startled him and then a large, horned
goat skittered past, followed by a pair of smaller goats and
then, moments later, an old man, tapping a crook. Seeing Fahad, he darted away after his herd, waving his stick at them.

Fahad called out to him and then hurried round the side
of the house to find him next to a pile of rubble, shooing
one of the smaller goats who had climbed onto the pile and
refused now to come down.

The man began speaking in a thin, high voice, so rapidly that Fahad could not follow everything he was saying. 'If
there is no one here,' the man cried out, knocking the bricks
with his stick, tottering it up the pile, 'what's the harm?'

'There's no harm,' Fahad said. But where was the sahib
of the house?

'There's no sahib,' the man said. 'No one has been here
a long time. Not since I was young. There was an old family
here. An important family.'

Fahad gave Ali's name.

'There was a tragedy,' the man said, 'and they left. Left
everything, all this land, a valuable petrol pump as well.'

'What was the tragedy?' Fahad wanted to know. But now
the goat had skipped off the pile of bricks and the man followed, raising his stick in salaam without looking back.

Fahad stood awhile in the forecourt. There was no breeze.
Nothing moved. He listened for the beat of his heart, for his
short, sharp breaths, to know that time was still passing.

The house was a ruin. How could he have failed to notice?

He imagined cars and trucks lined up out here. He imagined a charpayee in the shade of a tree, a servant dozing, another smoking a cigarette, he imagined Ali's voice calling to him—how loud Ali could be without shouting.

Then, he drove out to find the old Shell pump. Of course, why hadn't he thought of it himself?

It turned out that he had passed the pump on the way to the house without noticing. It was back along the main road. But now there were tall palms all around it, sheltering it from that busy highway like an oasis.

An attendant reluctantly took Fahad to an office at the back and introduced him to the owner, a Hindu who had bought the pump not so long ago. 'This you cannot lose money on,' he told Fahad, in English. 'Why they sold it I don't know.' He had a number for them, he said. Of course he did. He scrolled through his phone a long time before finding it and showing it to Fahad on the screen.

He asked after Fahad's father. He was unwell, people said. He didn't come anymore. They were selling the house, he'd heard. They were selling the lands. Was it true? 'I never thought this day would come, when your family would leave Abad. What is Abad? It is the place of your family.' Then he complained about the government, about the local politicians. 'One big difference,' he said, holding up a finger, 'your father didn't want money. These people, all they want is to make money, hand over fist, fist over hand.' He gestured as though he were reeling in a rope.

Fahad parked his car a short way down the road from the pump, along a train track. He looked at the phone number for a while, his eyes travelling across the digits as though they were a distance to cross, before dialling finally.

The phone rang and rang, rang so long he thought there must be no one home, and then a woman answered. 'Who?' she said, when he asked for Ali. He asked again and then the line went silent. After a moment, a child in the background began to cry.

'Hello?' Fahad said. 'Hello?'

Now a man's voice answered.

He was looking for Ali, Fahad said.

Who was it? the man asked.

Fahad gave his name. There was no response, and he gave his name again.

'Brother,' the man said slowly. Where was he calling from?

'From Abad,' Fahad said. He was an old friend. He'd come after many years. He'd passed by the pump and wondered. He'd stopped there and they'd given him the number. Was it the wrong number?

'It's been twenty, thirty years,' the man said. The child cried louder now. The man shouted at the child to stop, his voice suddenly certain, suddenly familiar.

'Ali?' Fahad said.

'Who else?' Ali said.

The child's voice became faint, and there were the sounds of footsteps and then a door slamming. 'You're in Abad?' Ali said. 'I thought, he'll never return, the way you left. I thought, once he's in America he'll stay there. In his heart, he's a foreigner. Once his father is old, the house, the lands, someone else will take it, I thought.'

Why had he left? Fahad wanted to know. Why had they sold everything? 'You said always, "Why would I go anywhere else? I have everything I want here."'

'Did I?'

'Everywhere I look,' Fahad said, 'I think of the places we'd go, the things we'd do.'

'Yes?' Ali said. 'It's good to remember.'

There was, from somewhere nearby, the sound of metal striking metal, chiming again, again, again.

'And you?' Ali said. 'One day you were there, then you were gone. Cruel as death. What has his father done, I thought.' The line crackled. The line buzzed. 'But they said, no, no, he's gone away is all.' Another voice tripped briefly, unintelligibly across the line.

Fahad asked after Ali's family. Who had answered the phone? he asked. Who was the child crying?

'The way you would talk of your father,' Ali said. 'But for you people it is different. You take what you want. Why shouldn't you?'

But why had he left? Fahad asked again. Why had they sold everything, the land, the pump?

The child howled in the background. 'Ask your father,' Ali said.

What was it to do with him, Fahad said. 'His mind is gone. He remembers little.'

'God works in strange ways,' Ali said, 'when he allows a man like that to forget the things he's done.'

He had looked for Ali here, Fahad said, amongst the people he saw on the roadside, amongst the visitors at the house. 'One moment in your life can cast such a long shadow.'

'Yes?' Ali said.

In the rearview mirror, Fahad thought for a moment that he saw him—his thick brow, his dark eyes flashing—but no, it was only his own reflection.

'Once,' Ali continued, 'once or twice, a few times, I went

to your lands. I drove around. "As if he's dead," I told myself. "Think of him like this."'

Those words were like rocks striking Fahad at his centre.

His wife was Punjabi, Ali said. That was why he'd come to Multan. If you come, you can see, he said, but when will you come? Never.

AHEAD, IN THE SHADE of a wall, a man hoicked up his kurta and squatted. The light had an unsettling clarity to it, as though Fahad had woken suddenly, and he lowered the sun visor across the windscreen.

What had his father done? He remembered those last days in Abad in a strange rush of sensation—the bitter taste of the syrup on his sundae at the Greenland Hotel, the dirt between his toes and against the backs of his knees, the wind whipping at his shirt, a smoke of chaff in the air, a horn bleating like a goat.

He wanted to remember what it had felt like with Ali, how it had been that afternoon in the copse. He could see them upon the forest floor, their dark limbs sinuous as snakes amongst the undergrowth, he could see the sky glimmer between the branches, he could hear the wind soughing through the leaves, but at a distance from himself, an unbridgeable distance. He remembered though, how quickly the feeling had twisted into something else, into something ugly, though it hadn't been, it hadn't been ugly at all.

They had returned by plane, he remembered the urgency of it, pictured him and his father on the Fokker, an empty seat between them, their eyes hard as stones. And in Karachi, he remembered his mother holding him by his shoulders. 'Is it?' he remembered her saying. 'Is it?' Again and again and again, and the only feeling he felt now, that he remembered feeling, was wanting never to see his own face again.

He returned home by another route, a track that led between lean-tos and along an open sewer and when the house came into view, he stopped the car for a moment. The avenue of trees had been here, the track curving between them. There had been an arch. He examined the ground for any sight of it, finding not twenty feet ahead a squat pillar of plastered concrete jutting out like a leg, and then, in the short dry grass at the edge of the sewer a white rock that, when he kicked it over, was painted with an eye.

He brushed the dirt away from it with his thumb. He polished the flat surface of the stone with a corner of his shirt. The lashes were painted long and flicked up at the ends to sharp points. Walking to the middle of the track, Fahad held the eye up, imagining what it had seen, looking out over all who dared to pass, and then turned it back towards the house.

TWENTY

MANY HAD GATHERED in the yard. They crowded the driveway and verandah and lawn, women and children too, some wailing, some counting rosary beads. They clustered around him as he climbed out of the car. It only strengthened his resolve. 'There's no other way,' he said, and what business was it of theirs? 'You have your lives to get on with, and I have mine.'

But no—it wasn't about selling the farm, it was his father. He hadn't been found yet.

The shadows were lengthening, they said. Soon it would be dark. He'd been gone since Fajr, twelve hours at least. Perhaps he'd had nothing to drink, perhaps nothing to eat, perhaps his feet were bare, his soles rubbed raw by the dirt. Perhaps he had fallen somewhere no one could hear him.

Had they looked in the town? Fahad wanted to know. Had they asked people? Why were so many here at the house? They should be out looking.

There were many looking, they said. A hundred men at least, from this village or that.

They had little faith in him. Fahad could see the doubt in their eyes.

He could ask a friend of Sahib, they suggested, but this one was dead, and that one a drunkard, and a third had betrayed him.

PACING IN CIRCLES around the yard, the servants looking on at him, Fahad called Alex.

'Where are you?' Alex said. 'I can't make out what you're saying I called the number you left but nobody answers. It's a strange dial tone.'

'That's Karachi,' Fahad said. 'I'm at the farm.'

'You're doing what?'

'My father,' Fahad said, 'he's gone somewhere. Without saying. In the night.'

'So he's alright?' Alex said. 'It wasn't true then?'

'It was,' Fahad said. 'That's what I'm saying.'

There'd been snow, Alex said. In November! They'd finally fixed the lift. He might have to fly to Frankfurt the following week.

'My father,' Fahad said. 'He goes for walks in the night. He went and hasn't come back.'

'I can't hear you,' Alex said.

'I can hear you fine,' Fahad said.

'I have to take another call.'

'But I don't know what to do,' Fahad said.

'HE ISN'T HERE?' Fahad asked the servants. 'You're sure?' He led them through the rooms of the house, through the hallway, the guest room, the dining and drawing rooms, his father's bedroom, the kitchen, up across the landing through Fahad's room, out onto the terrace, then back down again, moving in a procession; he led them round the compound, opening every door, looking in every office, the gatekeeper's hut, the servants' quarters.

At the back of the house, there was a narrow gate that opened onto the lands. 'What about from here?' Fahad said.

But no, see, it was bolted from the inside—they showed him.

What was it used for? Fahad wanted to know.

For the servants who lived in the villages to come and go, they said.

How could they come in the mornings if it was bolted from the inside? he asked.

In the mornings it was not, only during the day, one said.

Only in the mornings, another said.

Only in the evenings, a third said.

Had anyone looked out on the lands? Fahad asked.

Now they were silent. Now they worried their sandals into the dirt and knotted their hands together.

'Well,' Fahad said. He unbolted the gate himself, shoved it open.

A path disappeared into the vegetation, criss-crossed with footprints, as though crowds had come and gone. But here, in the undergrowth, a slipper was found. Was it Sahib's? It could be. It was foreign, not local, someone said. Then it could only be Sahib's.

It was shown to Fahad. It had a thick pad and a brown leather strap that was worn to threads at the edges.

'It looks like,' Fahad said.

He despatched them in groups across the fields. 'Send word to the villages,' he told them. There was an hour still before it would be dark. The sky was umber. The air was still. The birds and crickets strangely silent.

The bearer and the gatekeeper's son accompanied Fahad. The son, a boy in his teens, with a thin beard of fine hair halfway down his chest, prayed loudly, sometimes angrily, it seemed.

'He could be anywhere,' Fahad said. 'We're only on the tracks. He could have stumbled into the fields.' Fahad gestured to one side into the dense undergrowth. Did his father know of the plan to sell Abad?

'"I'll go home," he said this to me many times,' the bearer said. 'But this is his home, isn't it?'

'It is,' Fahad said.

'He's made of steel,' the bearer said. 'There's no stronger man. "The lion," they call him still. "Here comes the lion."'

The light had dimmed and the edges of things had become uncertain. Fahad pictured his father in a dark grove, crumpled into a pale heap, his eyes silvery, the evening gathering over him like a shroud. He didn't want to but he felt something like worry, like terror, jag through him, as though he were responsible for his father.

'I haven't told my mother,' he said, speaking more to himself than anyone else.

'It's good,' the bearer said. 'What can she do?'

Fahad imagined the search continuing till dawn, he imagined returning to the house, congregating in the yard, his father's absence somehow everywhere, obstructing every thought, no matter which way his mind turned.

———————

THE TRACK ASCENDED up to the canal bank. They followed the bank in the direction of the lowering sun.

'We should think where he might go,' Fahad said.

'He gets no rest, a man like this,' the bearer said. 'Always favours for others. But where are they now? They think of him only when they need him.'

Ahead, the fields disappeared into shadow. The setting sun scattered light down the empty canal.

The boy prayed louder now, his voice carrying so that it was as though he were saying those words directly to Fahad, as though he were chanting, and now Fahad remembered the shrine he and his father had stopped at on the way from Karachi, he remembered reaching through the bars of that cage, and now he imagined it was his father inside, his father's head beneath the totem.

He knew where his father would go. 'This way—' Fahad skidded off the track into the tall grasses.

They had attacked his father from all sides, the bearer said. A man like him, how many were there in the country, in the world? They'd stolen the elections from him, time after time. Men his father had trusted had turned on him, complaining he did too little for them, that he did nothing at all. 'What else did Sir do but their work?' the bearer said. 'What do I do but make tea for them when they come with their requests?

'He was the chief of the tribe,' the bearer continued. 'How could they support someone else? But they did. A thug, who paid people off, who bought votes, whose men stood at poll stations with guns, who burnt down the stations where the votes went against him. Is this the way?'

It had become darker now, whether because the light had dimmed from the sky or the foliage was denser, Fahad didn't know.

'And this man who came to the house,' the bearer continued, 'he cut the water to your lands. People were killed. Your farmers too. But still he didn't allow the water. Your father filed cases. But these cases take thirty, forty years and still nothing happens. Your father went from this general to that, from this parliamentarian to that, with his hands like this'—he cupped his palms together like a bowl—'but they did nothing.'

Fahad thought again of the shrine, thought of its meaning as though his life were a story he were narrating to himself.

'For years and years, your father would go to this one and the other, telling them, "My crops are dying, my villagers are dying." But he didn't have the power. How quickly people forget who a man is.'

The vegetation became sparse and the track became rocky. It climbed and then levelled out on a plateau at the family graveyard where the marble tombstones glowed in the half-light.

'Is this the Other Sir?' Fahad said, pausing before a tombstone that was unfamiliar. It was shaped like a turban with a point at the top.

The bearer thought so, he said, looking doubtfully at the letters engraved upon it. The gatekeeper's son read the inscription and still Fahad wasn't sure.

Beyond his grandfather's mausoleum, something stirred,

something loomed out of the shadows, becoming, as he watched, enormous, and Fahad took a step back, a few steps, stumbling. The boy called out some words of prayer, his voice breaking.

A cattle bell rang. The boy shone the light of his phone wildly ahead. It was an old man and a pair of scrawny brown cows, who galloped away in the beam.

He cares for the graveyard, the bearer told Fahad. He asked the man if he'd seen Sahib.

'Sahib comes many times,' the old man said. 'He comes to pay his respects. Even if it is the hottest day, he comes. Even if it is raining, he comes. The most respect he pays to this.' He pointed at the tombstone that might have been Mousey's. 'Even more than his father.' He wandered towards it and brushed his hand across it, wiped its edges with a grubby cloth that hung round his neck. 'When a man is alone,' he said, 'his life is here.' He climbed carefully between the graves to a place upon a bluff extending over the fields. 'This,' the old man said, 'Sahib chose for himself.' The sun had set and only the lights of the town were visible, flickering in the distance like a line of ships.

He was dead. His father was dead and he knew it for certain. Fahad's legs buckled so that he found himself on his hands and knees on the stony earth, the air close and heavy. I forgive you, I forgive you, I forgive you, he thought, thinking even of what his father might have done to cause Ali to leave.

I forgive every step that led me here. He knew what it was to be alone because he was alone and he imagined undoing his life stitch by stitch so that the threads could be woven another way, so that this end, which was knotted into his destiny from his first moment in this place, could be unknotted.

He scrabbled at the dirt, some clumps pliable as mud, others hard as rock, gripped them in his fists so that the edges might cut him.

Only today, the old man continued, only hours earlier, Sahib had come, had stood looking out across the lands. '"The sun is too hot," I told him. But he stayed a long while, at least till Asr.'

TWENTY-ONE

THE GATE WAS OPEN wide enough for Rafik to pass through. He called out—but with the sounds of the breeze rustling through the leaves of the fruit trees in the yard, a water pump ticking nearby, a cowbell, his voice was too quiet for even him to hear.

The porch was a short distance away and yet, as he moved towards it, it wobbled, receding, so that he became unsure he would reach it until his foot was on the lowest step, and then the next, and then the next.

The front door was locked. He banged. He rattled the door in its hinges. Then, he sat on the steps and realised he did not want to get up again, that perhaps he could not.

The air was smoky with dusk and he remembered the lightness of being a child, how buoyant youth was, how easy to skip along these very paths, to chase after stray goats, to bounce stones off the earthen village walls pocked with dung.

He heard the throttle of a scooter engine and saw a front tyre nosing its way through the gap in the gate. The man parked the scooter by a gatekeeper's hut. He unwound a plastic bag from the handlebars, frowned into it, cradled its weight in his palm.

He spat against the wall, a stream thick as a rope and red as blood. He would have passed round to the back of the house, had Rafik not called out to him.

Something fell from the bag—a tomato—and tumbled away.

'Who is it?' the man said, and motioned at Rafik as though he might strike him. 'What do you want? Why are you here?'

Rafik attempted to stand and, gripping a baluster, managed to. 'You bastard,' he said. 'You come here and I'll give you a slap. Where's your master?'

The man moved nearer, squinting at Rafik. 'Who is it?' he said again, but a little more gently. Then after a strange pause, 'Sir?' He tilted his head to one side, then the other like a bird. Suddenly, he darted forward. 'Sir, I didn't recognise you.' He reached down to touch Rafik's feet. 'Has something happened? Your clothes—' he said. 'Your—' He gestured at his own face. 'Has something happened?' he said again.

'Idiot,' Rafik said, reaching towards the man's arm to steady himself. 'Where's Sahib?'

The man shook his head. 'Sahib?' he said.

'You can't hear?' Rafik indicated that he wanted to go into the house.

'The door is locked from the inside,' the man said. He unclasped Rafik's fingers from his arm and placed them upon the doorframe. 'I'll go round,' he said, and then jogged down the steps. The bag he had carried lay by a post, tomatoes spilling out of it, one rolling off the edge of the porch into a bush below.

A bolt loosened inside the house, then the door clattered

and shook and dust rose from its screen and hinges. It swung open and the man helped Rafik in.

'Why is it so dark?' Rafik said. The man parked him in the hallway and hurried around raising blinds, throwing curtains open, so that the space could be seen.

Rafik discovered that he was very thirsty, his throat so parched words caught in his mouth. The man brought him a glass of lukewarm water.

'This'—Rafik indicated a photograph on the wall—'is a girl his father wanted him to marry, her father was a highly respected civil servant'—then another—'this is my uncle's old Plymouth. It was fire engine red. Not another car like it in the country.' There was a very large photograph of his uncle— 'this is his desk when he was chief minister, it's written over here—' He followed the letters with his fingertip. By the door to the drawing room, there was a smaller photograph— 'my engagement,' Rafik said, tapping the glass. 'How angry she was that day. She threw the ring. She said, "You and the dogs you call your family can go to hell. To hell." That's what she said. She has her own way.'

He signalled up the stairs. 'He's there?' Rafik said. 'He's resting? The old so-and-so. He's lazy. He should be out look- ing after his lands. They'll fleece him, these tillers and man- agers, if they know he's never around.'

The man took the empty glass from him, which Rafik had forgotten he was holding.

Rafik wandered into the drawing room. 'And why is this furniture covered up?' Rafik said. 'People will think the house is empty, that no one comes, no one lives here.'

'Yes, sir,' the man said. He folded back the sheets across

the sofas, swiped at the cushions, raising clouds of dust from them.

An odd sort of tiredness came over Rafik. He sat. 'Call him now, even if he's sleeping, you tell him his brother has come, wake him.' The man remained where he was—between a side table and an armchair. 'Your boss,' Rafik continued, 'he's a clever man. But he doesn't look after himself. You look after him. I'll give you something.' He reached for his pocket—and found that he had no pockets by his hips, that he was in his pyjamas. 'Oh,' he said. There was a breast pocket but it was empty. His feet were bare, and, as he looked down he saw that one of his soles was black with dirt, a pebble embedded in the heel. 'How I've come here.'

'Sir,' the man said, 'there's a cut.' He drew a line across his own temple to show Rafik where. 'I'll clean it.' He brought a basin of hot water, a cloth, some Dettol. He dabbed the cloth gently at Rafik's face.

'I have a son now,' Rafik said. 'He's too much here.' He rapped his knuckle against the side of his head. 'He makes himself unhappy. But here'—he held his knuckle at his temple—'he is not alone, at least. He is not lost.'

When he had finished, the man said, cradling the bowl against his chest, 'Sahib is not in the house. Shall I call for your car?'

'Where is he?' Rafik said. He tried to stand, but his body had an impossible weight to it that anchored him down, his head lolling back against a cushion. 'Where does he go? He doesn't go anywhere. He's here. Where else?'

'Sir,' the man said, 'it's been twenty years now.' He dipped his face into the steam rising from the water in the bowl.

'Whatever happened, it's a family matter,' the man said, 'but he spoke your name often, he spoke about you and your son often.'

'You tell him—' Rafik said, half remembering now, half remembering that Mousey, Mousey was gone. Mousey was gone. 'You tell him,' Rafik said again.

The room sparkled with dust. He reached his fingers out and made the dust dance in the low beams of light that angled through the windows. 'We're children, and we think we are gods.'

It was quiet there, so quiet it was as if life had stopped a moment, and there was this extraordinary relief in it and then he made the dust motes dance again and then there was the sound outside of the cowbell, there was the sound of a goat bleating. The light now struck the glass of a picture frame on the table, a point of light so sharp he had to shield his eyes, he had to look away.

'I only have the scooter,' the man said, 'or I'd take you to your house. But I'll call them.'

'If my father is angry,' Rafik said, 'you say something, say I was with Mousey, say we had learnt our lesson but the maulvi sahib didn't come, tell him or he'll beat us both.'

TWENTY-TWO

THE HEADLIGHTS WERE so weak they illuminated only a foot of track ahead of the jeep, the branches, stalks and leaves and their shadows reaching quite suddenly at the windscreen, sticks and stones crunching under the tyres.

The driver took a wrong turn and had to reverse up a narrow path blindly, Fahad certain they'd tip into a ditch, they'd tumble into the canal, they might even be up on the bank, who knew precisely where they were? But the driver corrected himself and came to a halt. He sounded his horn and then climbed out of the car. He could not open the gate, he said. Earth was piled up against it. But he showed Fahad a gap large enough to pass through on foot.

Ahead, a window was lit in the house, a large square of warm, copper light. There was a cabinet against a wall, a sofa, and armchairs, and was that the back of someone's head?

He banged on the door. A man opened it. He led Fahad through a hallway into a drawing room to the left.

Though Fahad was looking directly at him, he did not see his father till the man stirred and glanced up.

He was tiny, bundled into his clothes, which were streaked with dirt and ragged, a flap torn open to reveal a pale shoulder. His cheeks were stubbled with white hair and his eyes were sunken.

'You gave us a scare,' Fahad said, 'wandering off. It's me, it's Fahad,' he added.

'Fahad,' his father said, as though to himself, narrowing his eyes into the middle distance. 'Fahad,' he said again.

'Fahad,' Fahad said. What else could he say?

The manservant who had welcomed him in called out loudly over his shoulder, as though his father were deaf, 'It's your son, your son has come, he was worried.'

'Yes, yes,' his father said, sitting up now, leaning against the armrest as though to stand. 'Worried why? Always worrying. Like an old woman.'

The man hurried towards his father to help him but his father batted him away.

'You know who this is?' his father said. He grabbed at the man's collar, steadying himself. The hems of his pyjamas pooled at his bare feet, his toenails caked with mud. 'This is the boy who cared for Mousey. Mousey drank and drank. He could be difficult. You didn't see it. This man stayed right till the end.'

'You came to this house when you were a child,' the man said to Fahad.

'He wouldn't leave him even at night. He slept in a cot at the foot of Mousey's bed.' His father gestured at the man. 'Show him,' he said.

'Yes, sir?' the man said.

'I wondered where you were,' Fahad said. 'You didn't say. I didn't know what to tell Mummy.'

'I have to take permission like a child when I go?' his father said, and then swiped out as if he'd slap someone away. 'Your uncle said to me, he said, "Look after this boy when I'm gone," he wrote it in his will to me, that this boy should have something. He said, "This boy cared for me, he's my family, think of him as my family." Then, "I've asked you only one thing in my life before." He'd wanted me to speak to our fathers so he shouldn't be sent away. But what could I do? I was a child myself. "This is my second, my last request. When no one would care for me, this boy has cared." He had died. What could I say? I said to this boy, he'll tell you, "As long as I am here"'—his father pointed at the ground—'"this house shall be yours to live in, no one dare disturb you from here." Didn't I say this?' He directed this question at the man, who tilted his head like he was nodding. 'Show him,' Fahad's father said, 'upstairs.'

The man hesitated a moment. Then he guided Fahad back through the hallway and up a staircase. There were photographs along the wall—several studio pictures in black and white of a rakish, dashing Mousey.

'He looks like a hero,' the man said, slowing in front of a particular photograph. 'He sang beautifully. He would sing songs from the movies. Some mornings we would sing together—he did one part, I did the other—though, it's true, he preferred to sing alone.'

At the top of the stairs, there was a door off a landing, and the man opened it then switched on a light. There was a bed and at the foot of it a narrow cot perpendicular to it. The bed was neatly made, with a mosquito net tucked over its edges. The cot had a local quilt draped across it with a pattern of lines radiating from the centre and a bolster cushion for a pillow.

'I should have been a teacher,' the man said. 'In the whole province, I came first in the exam. I should have gone to the city. There was a very good job. The best.' He gave the name of a school Fahad didn't know. 'By now I would have a family, a car, a home, I would take holidays. But'—he gestured at the bed—'your uncle came from abroad. He needed a man with some English. My father said to me, "You're clever. You'll learn. And he is an elder—"' He shrugged. 'Now this house is a mausoleum. And someone must care for it.'

Fahad remembered seeing the man when he was younger, remembered seeing him here in this house, and it was a memory still with too much heat to hold in the forefront of his mind.

'When you were a boy,' the man continued, 'you would go to the hotel for ice cream, you had a friend.'

On the side table, there was a photograph. Fahad tilted it under the light. It was Mousey and this man in front of that funny Kermit green jeep Mousey had out on the canal bank, the two of them leaning towards each other, slender as children, Mousey shielding his eyes from the sun so that a shadow fell across his face, a breeze tugging a lock of hair loose from the top of his head, curling it up like a question mark. Fahad thought of all the years he'd been away, of how different things could have been and Riaz, that was the man's name, Fahad remembered it all of a sudden, Riaz seeing Fahad's face said, 'He spoke of you often. He thought of you as a son almost. He said, "He'll come back. One day, he'll come."'

Fahad turned away and stared into a corner of the room.

'Such men,' Riaz continued, 'there are few like that. Your father is the same.'

THEY DID NOT SPEAK for a while once in the jeep. Fahad drove, not wanting to sit in the back, but in the rearview mirror he could see the driver staring at his father, at the cut on his temple, the grazes on his cheek, his wild, wild hair and torn collar.

'You let that man stay in Mousey's house as though it's his?' Fahad said. He didn't mean it as a challenge though perhaps it sounded like that.

'Baba, he was Mousey's friend, he was like a son to him or a brother even. It was Mousey's wish. Should I say no? Throw him out on his behind?'

'No,' Fahad said.

'I must show some respect to Mousey. What is love but the things we do if they know or not? When I go to my father's grave, it is love even if he cannot see it.'

'I'll have to go back soon,' Fahad said. 'Not tomorrow, but the morning after.'

His father nodded slowly. 'To where?'

'Karachi. Then, London.'

His father nodded again. The car rattled over a deep divot, and he steadied himself against the armrest. 'You haven't seen my files. That I want you to do. It's a project for you.'

He'd look, Fahad said. 'You won't be able to come back and forth, between Abad and Karachi,' he said. 'And these people are running the farm into the ground.'

'They know nothing,' his father said. 'Incompetent.'

'They are.'

The headlights flickered and then dimmed further so that they were driving almost in the dark, and yet the path unfurled ahead of them like a carpet.

'If you were here,' his father said, and he gestured around them where the fields must have been.

'Yes.'

'A lot you could do,' his father said.

'Yes,' Fahad said.

Suddenly the headlights blazed as they sped up the incline onto the canal bank and then rattled along it, scraps on the canal bed glinting like glass.

'I was a boy here,' his father said. 'Mousey and I, we'd run around dirty as the village children, playing cricket on the sward between the harvests, swimming when the canal was full. We had our friends here—this farmer you've seen with the funny lip, he was a bowler. His brother was a batsman.' The track became broad. 'I learnt to drive.' He jabbed his hand towards the seat well. 'I drove into the ditch, like you did, and they came, ten farmers, to pick the car up, it was an old Plymouth, to carry it onto the road.'

They crossed over a narrow bridge and his father waved that he should stop. He climbed out of the car. There was a full moon and the land was still. His father stood in a column of light. A gust of wind tugged at his torn clothes and at his bright white hair, but he himself seemed immovable. 'How much the mind can carry,' he said. 'All this.' And he swept his arm across that view.

TWENTY-THREE

THE NEXT MORNING, Fahad called his mother.

'Is it done?' she said.

'You'll have to find someone else,' he said. 'I can't.'

'Find who?' she said. 'Should I do it myself?' She sounded wild. 'The roof has fallen. In the drawing room. This is how I live. Should I die like this too? All because you and your father are cowards? Too sentimental? And for what? What is the place to you? Or to him? It's land. That is all. It's dirt. And it will stay that way. With you or without.'

'He'll never allow it,' he said. Then, 'The roof?'

'You'll see,' she said. 'The birds are inside. Your father will be happy. When the house is on top of my head, your father will be happy.'

'There's no time now,' Fahad said. 'Another time.'

'I'm finished,' his mother said. 'I'm done. I gave my life in this. In what? In this. Picking up after spoilt children. You did as you wanted. You made a mess and you went and you stayed away, doing God knows what. You keep yourself happy.' She said it as though it were a curse.

———

HE WANTED TO BE GOOD. He wanted to be gone. He wanted to remember nothing. He wanted no time to pass at all and he wanted so much time to pass that none of this mattered anymore. He wandered from room to room. It wasn't sentimentality.

He had his father's files dusted off and laid out across the dining table. What did he think was in them? What did he plan to do? Did he expect to find an answer in them? An answer to what he should do now or an answer to who his father was to him, an answer to who Fahad was himself, an answer to what had happened and whether it mattered at all.

THE FILES WERE in no particular order. He set the first in front of him and flipped it open. The front page was illegible, crinkled and streaked with ink. The next page was the same. And the next. He turned them quickly, and they were so brittle that the edges crumbled. In some places the ink had disappeared altogether, in others, smudges and daubs remained. Here and there he could decipher phrases: the seal of the air marshall, several words X-ed out in type, 'in anticipation of a favourable.'

Of course, it had rained before he'd travelled from Karachi. They'd loaded the car in a torrential downpour. Was there nothing here at all?

The next file was in even worse condition, the one after that marginally better. A letter was intact—from a furniture designer for the refurbishment of a guest room. A subsequent file was barely damaged, and yet he flicked rapidly through internal memoranda from his father's days in the foreign ministry—notes on Carter ('in fine fettle'), Ceauşescu ('witty'), Thatcher ('judgement?')—without much interest.

His father appeared suddenly at the threshold to the dining room. 'It is here,' his father said, striking the air with his finger. The barber had been sent for to tidy him, and he'd dressed in a bright white starched kurta, so he looked now quite unlike how he had the night before, as slender and imperious as one of the herons that gathered in the sodden fields during the paddy season. 'Isn't it?'

WHAT DID IT MATTER, the history of a country? What did it matter that Simla might have been different but for his father, that Kargil might have been different? What did it matter that Saddam's favourite son was the third, or that Reagan's father was a salesman, or that Gaddafi had planned to escape to Jeddah? It mattered, of course it mattered. It changed the course of people's lives. Hadn't his father's ambition changed the course of his?

And yet, what interested him was not his father's politics— his father had none, his politics were himself, like any other man of ambition—what interested Fahad was something he found in one of the last files he looked at, a slender folder wrapped so many times in plastic that it seemed to be nothing until he unwrapped it.

It was marked 'personal.' It contained a few dozen pages, a message from his father's tailor, another from the Club, a perfunctory note from his mother with a list of the house staff and their salaries. There was a large brown manila envelope at the back of the folder. He emptied it out onto the table. There were passport pictures of Fahad at various ages: here he was no more than four or five, here he was perhaps a year old, being held up by disembodied arms, here he was in his teens, maybe when he'd left Pakistan. There were letters too that appeared to be from him to his father, that were in his hand and signed with his name, but were entirely unfamiliar.

One was a curt request for money: 'that I should have to ask,' 'but it really isn't enough,' 'of course you're happy to put me in the position.' Another was longer, almost conversational.

'Regarding your letter,' he had written, 'I don't know why you think I should care at all. I barely remember the place or the people. You don't say what it is that this fellow has done, only that he has had the temerity to run against you. In the elections, I suppose you mean, as that is all there is for you. Just to remind you, his father was closer to you than the son was to me. I was there only a few months. I barely knew him. It surprises me though that the fellow should oppose you. I thought his father was a great supporter of yours. Have you spoken to him about this? Or are you just planning to bulldoze him and everything of his because he's challenged you? And as for organising rallies, well, maybe the people have something to demonstrate about. Have you thought of that? Or listened to what they have to say? It is supposed to be a democracy, isn't it? They are supposed to have a voice, aren't they? Maybe he has listened to them, and that's why they're following him? If that's the case, then just getting rid of him won't solve the problem. But if that's what you want to do, if you're looking for an excuse to do that, to banish him, don't hold back on my account. Don't consider me at all. That will be easy. And you can let "the people" know, whoever they are, that I will never come back so there's no sense in wishing it.'

He drew his fingertip across the page, as if there were other meanings to be found there. As he was reading, as he began to understand whom the letter referred to, his heartbeat quickened and he felt his face become hot.

There was another letter in a different hand, a scrawl so wild the letters were difficult to decipher. He skipped to the end—it was signed 'S'—and then back to the start.

'Why now a bank? There is this mill and that, the cotton gins, the flour, the textiles, and you have no interest in running them, only setting them up and even that you have someone else do, no doubt at great cost, so that you can return as quickly as possible to Islamabad. You are too busy with these generals and ministers to manage this [illegible]. And what happens to empires? Like the men who build them, they die too. You cannot trust these rogues—and they all are, you can't see it, but they are. I'd rather trust that rat, your cousin, than any of these scoundrels. And of course, who it should be is your son. Put your pride aside for once, for once, and bring him back. His studies are over now, he has no excuse to stay. And what caused him to want to leave, well we must confront it, we must acknowledge it, whether we want to or not, we must, or [illegible]. He was a boy, we shouldn't have allowed it. We should have said no. But you did not, because perhaps you thought he was right, that he should go, that this was no place for him. Well you must fix that. You must—or what is there of this family? And you will see, one day you will see, that it's all you have, that there is nothing else, all these hangers-on will disappear one day, all this power will be gone, and then you will see.'

HE REREAD THIS ONCE, twice, again, doubling back over certain phrases, his finger unsteady as it moved across the page. 'Is it what you want?' he remembered his mother saying, as she held him by his shoulders, her eyes sparkling. 'Is it? Is it?' He remembered leaving Abad, refusing to look back, gritting his teeth so hard pain jagged up his temples, remembered wanting, more than anything he'd ever wanted, with a terrible, fierce longing, to leave a part of himself, the worst part, the most inescapable part of himself, in Abad.

HE STOOD AWHILE out on the terrace, up on the ledge, watching the shadows lengthen. The wild grasses surged and dipped like waves, a froth of tiny white flowers for surf here and there. The copse was a dark shadow that wobbled and wavered like something submerged, and his mind bobbed unsteadily towards it. He had buried the memory beneath a riot of memories, purposely jumbling them, one over the other, purposely confusing the way that they felt, so that an inexplicable blood-rushing desire rippled through shame and anger. He felt fierce and pathetic, cunning and stupid, so that it seemed to him now, as he excavated those memories, as he unmuddled scenes, tugged one loose from another, that he had lured Ali to that place, he had collapsed Ali into his desire, and then he had sloughed him away. It seemed to him now that he had banished himself from this place, he had banished himself from himself, that he was the villain.

MUSTAFA WAS ANNOUNCED a little before Maghrib. So.

Fahad worried there might be a crowd to witness it all, but it was only him and an ancient bearded man Mustafa introduced as the registrar. The registrar carried a large worn book bound in red cloth, tied with a strip of white muslin, the sort given to servants for Edh outfits. He stroked his beard, even as he bowed hello, even as he shook Fahad's hand.

They sat in the drawing room, bent over a coffee table where the registrar opened the book and set out various documents. The pages of the book were handwritten in the style of a ledger.

There were terms to be agreed to. Mousey's old house, it turned out, was no longer in Rafik's name. Rafik had gifted it away. 'This man who lives there,' the registrar said, 'it belongs to him now.'

'Your father did many things,' Mustafa said, 'odd things. Now someone will take better care.'

Fahad and Mustafa argued over the rate and what exactly it would include, Fahad not caring how poorly he spoke the language, how shrill his voice became, agreeing finally on a price that made Mustafa demonstrably uncomfortable, made him pause, turn away, excuse himself to make a call, eventually agreeing that they could have till the end of the month to clear the house, and that they could keep the graveyard. The deeds were amended by hand. The registrar slid them in front of Fahad, indicating with an X here and another there where Fahad's father would need to sign.

'He may not do it,' Fahad said, and a part of him hoped his father would not.

'If a son asks, how will a father say no?' Mustafa said, interlocking his fingers, steepling them beneath his chin.

The registrar suggested coyly that the signatures need only appear to be his father's, that the purpose of the signatures was to communicate that the family committed. Who was there after his father but Fahad after all? Fahad could take the ledger, could take the deed to his father. They'd accept his word that the signatures were his father's. Theirs was the oldest family, the man said. Their family, their word, was second only to God's word.

'Still,' Fahad said, and he collected the papers loosely together.

His father's room was empty, though the bedside lamp between the tables was lit. No—there his father was, sitting on the carpet beneath the lamp, the lamplight pooling over him, the news spread out over his knees.

'Come,' his father said. He patted the bed. 'Sit.'

Fahad sat.

There was a strange, wonderful ease to being there, the two of them still as insects in amber, so that he wanted it to stay like this always, so that he wondered why it hadn't been like this before.

His foot rested upon his father's—and how similar they were, indistinguishable really, but for the white hair scattered upon the bridge of his father's foot. He wondered what his father would have done were he in Fahad's position and imagined suddenly the two of them hand in hand walking along the canal bank, the sun low ahead, the canal brimming with water.

'We go here, we go there,' his father said, 'and what is it really? Is it any different? Or is it here—' He tapped his finger to his chest.

'Do you remember a lot,' Fahad said, 'about the place?' meaning Abad.

His father nodded. 'A little,' he said. 'Sometimes you don't know what you remember and what you think you remember. Sometimes, even my father's face, when I remember it, it is one way, sometimes another. But what is there to be afraid of? A man is more than his face. He is more than the places he has been. And the places he has been, they are in here' — again he tapped his chest—'nowhere else. We carry it where we go. Everything. What does it mean to leave?' he said. 'We can only leave ourselves.' Looking at Fahad, his eyes were silvery. 'You're a good boy. You're tough.' He clenched his fist. 'You think you're too soft. But you have your mother's—' He shook his fist. 'She has lived through everything. At the end of the world, she'll be standing, still. She doesn't show it. The earth shakes, and she, she is immovable. The roof stays up, only because the pillars are strong.'

What were the papers in Fahad's hands? he asked. 'You need me to sign?' His father reached blindly behind him for a pen on the bedside table. He patted the newspaper across his knees. Fahad set the ledger on his father's lap, pointed at the X.

His father carefully signed across the first page, and then the second, without reading. He shut the papers into the ledger, returned it to Fahad.

'You need me to come?' he said.

Fahad shook his head.

'Good.' His father nodded.

AFTER THE DEED had been signed, after Mustafa and the registrar had departed, Fahad summoned all the servants to the drawing room. Some sat on the carpet around him, some stood.

He wanted to tell them that the house and land had been sold, that they would be dismissed at the end of the month, that the contents of the house should be packed and sent to Karachi, but he found himself unable to. Finally, the bearer said, 'We know. Today, Abad is gone. What remains is land, is earth, is water and air, but it is not Abad.'

Fahad and his father left early the next morning, as dawn was breaking. The older servants had gathered to see them off, the bearer helping his father into the car, the cook tucking a loose corner of his father's kurta inside so that it would not be shut in the door, the gatekeeper shutting the car door so gently it barely made a sound.

The house was quiet, the windows shuttered. Beyond the wall, even the noise of the town had abated. There was no breeze. The sky was clear. The air was hot. His father looked only ahead, signalled that the gate should be opened, that the driver should proceed.

The verandah was empty. The yard was empty. The fields were hidden behind the back wall.

'I'll look,' Fahad said, gesturing towards the little gate that led out there.

'We're waiting,' his father said.

From the back gate, there was no great vista. The bracken was too tall, the trees too close. But the leaves had their own sound, the dry grasses, the earth. He crouched, scrabbled for a handful of dirt and held it up: dry, sharp stones, a fine powder of chaff, a broken twig. The horn sounded, startling herons from a distant field. They swooped low overhead, flashing their silver wings, and then away.

TWENTY-FOUR

THE BOY WAS in a strange mood, pressing his face to the window like a child for most of the journey, smudging the glass with his nose.

Rafik slept and woke, slept and woke. He found no pleasure in sleep anymore. Once it had been a sweet, cool respite like prayer, but now he drifted in and out of it so that waking was like sleeping and sleeping like waking, so that one place was like another, so that eating, hearing, feeling were like each other and like nothing at all. The only sweetness still was in the mind.

Did Rafik remember, the boy wanted to know, their last trip to Abad?

'I'm an old man,' Rafik said.

Did he remember, the boy continued, a friend of his in Abad, a young fellow, they'd been inseparable.

'Yes,' Rafik said, 'you made a good friend.'

His father had been a landlord, the boy said, a little farm off the bypass to Baluchistan. They'd had a petrol pump.

'Well remembered,' Rafik said.

What had become of them? Fahad said. Their farm had been sold, the house abandoned. They'd moved away.

'That I don't know,' Rafik said. They could find out, they could ask people.

It was in the files he'd given, Fahad continued. 'Ali challenged you. He tried running against you.'

'Possible,' Rafik said. And then, 'These little fellows, they come up and they think something of themselves. You have to—' He pressed the tip of his thumb against a spot in the air, jiggled it side to side, as though he were squashing a fly.

'Anyone who's in the way,' Fahad said. 'As easy as that.' He swiped his hand like a blade, knocking into one headrest, then the other. 'But for what?'

'For what?' Rafik said. The sun was bright in his eyes and he flipped the visor down.

'What do you have to show?' Fahad said, sitting forward.

'You keep a dog to guard the house, and when he barks, you'—he joined his hands together—'you say forgive me, I had no idea, but you're happy you are safe. You and your mother, you do as you like, spend money like it's water, but where does the money come from? "Don't tell me," you say, and you look away like a shy bride.'

'Money,' Fahad said. 'It's always the way.'

'I don't care a damn for it,' Rafik said. 'How do we go to the grave? Without even'—he gestured into the seat well at his slippers—'these.' He looked for the boy in the rearview mirror but the back seat was empty. 'Where is he?' He gripped the driver by the arm—'We've forgotten him—' But then, when Rafik turned to look again, it was Mousey twisted into the corner, in a gaudy shirt, chains round his neck and rings in his ear.

'Your son,' Mousey said. 'You threw him to the wolves. For land, for office, and look at you now.'

'He wanted to go,' Rafik said. 'He knew his mind. Like his mother, what they want they must have.'

'What does a child know?' Mousey said.

'Should I lock him up to stop him leaving?' Was the traffic speeding towards them now? Rafik threw his hands in front of him.

'I did it for you,' Mousey said. 'That was what I knew. You wanted me gone and I went.'

'Never—' Rafik tilted this way and that, to dodge this truck, this bus, this Hilux. 'What are you doing?' he shouted at the driver. 'You'll kill us.'

Mousey put his hand on Rafik's shoulder and shook it.

'I prayed that you'd return,' Rafik said. 'I prayed for it.'

TWENTY-FIVE

THEY REACHED KARACHI at nightfall, their bags carried in a hurried whisper into the house, as though there were something clandestine in their return.

His mother was sitting at the table in the courtyard, still as stone, staring out into the middle distance, seeming for a time not to register them at all.

His father patted her on the shoulder and then wandered out onto the terrace.

It was done, Fahad wanted to say, but could not.

'A place isn't nothing,' he said instead. 'It isn't like every other. There is something in the earth, in the walls—' Here he touched his palm to the hot plaster beside him.

'And people?' she said. 'Is there something there? Or is that nothing? Is this something?' She pinched the skin on her arm.

'Why are you always fighting?' he said. 'You got what you wanted, but even still. Isn't it exhausting? Aren't you tired?'

'I would like to sleep and not wake up,' she said. 'Then

you'd be free. You could do what you wanted with all these things.' She gestured around her.

'I don't want to argue,' Fahad said.

She reached up, took his hand in hers. 'We had gone to China, your father and I. He was meeting Deng. They take the women shopping, to buy jewellery and things like this. I wanted to see the Forbidden City. There was an old woman sitting on the ground. Completely white hair. Maybe she was blind even. But she wanted to hold my hand. She felt the lines on my palm. She read my fortune. There was a translator because I didn't understand. "You will live a long life," she said. "Very good," I said. Then she said something else. The translator didn't tell me. I had to ask. "Ma'am, it is not always good," she said. "It is like a curse to live so long."'

He squeezed her fingers. 'You've never told me that,' he said.

'You haven't been here,' she said. 'You bring who you want. If you have a friend, someone you live with, bring him. What do we care? You think it is us, looking over your shoulder, that it is us shaking our heads at the things you do.'

'Even if it was me,' he said to his mother, 'shaking my head at the things I did, I didn't come from nowhere. I came from somewhere. Even if it was me.' And he wondered now if he had been found out in the copse that summer, or if he had only found out himself.

'THE ROOF!' he remembered suddenly, and asked about the drawing room.

His mother waved the question away. 'I managed,' she said. 'I had it attended to.'

Fahad wanted to see. His mother let him go alone.

He couldn't see much the matter with it except in a far corner of the ceiling a cloudy brown stain and on the sofa beneath the stain a dark streak across the sofa's back. The cushions had been set aside in a stack. There were no cracks in the wall, no fresh paint, no fresh plaster.

'It looks alright,' he said when he returned to his mother in the courtyard, sitting down beside her.

She nodded. 'Lucky escape.'

'WHERE ARE THE BIRDS?' Rafik appeared in between the open doors to the terrace: pale, shirtless, silvery hair on his chest, an empty dish balanced upon his forearm.

'It's late,' Soraya said. 'It's the middle of the night. They'll be roosting. They'll come in the morning.'

He nodded, turned, slid the doors shut.

'Abad is gone,' she said. 'You understand that? It's finished.'

'No, no,' Rafik said. 'We were there. We just came from there.'

'Yes,' she said. 'But there's no going back.'

'The boy will tell you.' Rafik placed the dish on the table. He sat. 'We went together—father and son. The paddy was tall as a man. He'll tell you. Wasn't it? There'll be such a crop as you haven't seen. You can take him to London. You can buy all you want. You say I'm a miser, I give you no spending money. I'll give you thousands. I'll give you wads of it.' He held up those imaginary wads, shook them in his fist. 'The crisp new fifties you like. And you take him. To all these fancy restaurants, to see these plays and musicals. These are the things he likes.'

They, each of them, had spread their hands out across the table so that there were three pairs of hands, not so very different at all, the fingers touching at their tips.

'He read my papers.' Rafik nodded towards Fahad. '"It's all very interesting," he said.'

'I think I know,' Fahad said. 'I think I know who he is, who I am, who you are, and then I don't.'

'What does it matter?' Soraya said.

'He forgets and we should forget too'—Fahad stood up, kicking his chair away from the table so that it toppled—'the terrible things he did, the terrible things I did.'

'This is how you are,' Soraya said, 'you men. Breaking things, your own things even.'

'Aren't we accountable?' Fahad said. 'Shouldn't there be a ledger that says, he did this and I did that and you did this?'

'And then?' his mother said. 'You'll add it up?'

'Or how can I know?' Fahad said.

His mother reached for his hand, looped her fingers into his.

'That's what I'll write,' he said. 'I'll write it so we know— who you are, who you are—' He looked at his mother. 'Who I am.'

'And what will it be,' she said, 'only another story.'

One of the strip lights on the wall flickered, buzzed, went out, and came back on brighter.

ACKNOWLEDGEMENTS

Though a town called Abad exists in northern Sindh, the Abad in this novel is a version of nearby Jacobabad, where the Soomros have farmed land for generations. My grandfather Illahibukhsh took me to Jacobabad as a child and later taught me to farm. Like Rafik, he is a politician farmer, but there the similarity ends. Rafik has barely a fraction of my grandfather's brilliance, kindness, honour, and courage. Still, this novel is a tribute to my grandfather, to Jacobabad (despite my conflicted feelings for the place), to the years we have spent there together and elsewhere, before and since.

My thanks to Natasha Fairweather, who encouraged me from the start and has guided me so wisely through the publication process, and all at RCW; to Adam Eaglin; to Mitzi Angel for her very sensitive and careful edits; to Molly Walls and the rest of the team at FSG; to Kate Harvey for her support and all at Vintage; to Jean McNeil; to Deepa Anappara, who has been my sage this last decade; to my extraordinary cohort at UEA, from whom I learnt so much about writing; to my darling sisters, Tanya and Tara; and to Giambattista, whom I love dearly.

A NOTE ABOUT THE AUTHOR

Taymour Soomro is a British Pakistani writer. He studied law at Cambridge University and Stanford Law School. He has worked as a corporate solicitor in London and Milan, a lecturer at a university in Karachi, an agricultural estate manager in rural Sindh, and a publicist for a luxury fashion brand in London. His short fiction has appeared in *The New Yorker* and *The Southern Review*. He is the coeditor, with Deepa Anappara, of the forthcoming anthology *Letters to a Writer of Colour*.